COOLER HEADS

Books by Julian Tepper

Balls (2012)

Ark (2016)

Between the Records (2020)

Cooler Heads (2024)

JULIAN TEPPER

COOLER HEADS

a novel

RARE BIRD
LOS ANGELES, CALIF.

READ OR DIE

THIS IS A GENUINE RARE BIRD BOOK

Rare Bird Books
6044 North Figueroa Street
Los Angeles, CA 90042
rarebirdbooks.com

Copyright © 2024 by Julian Tepper

FIRST HARDCOVER EDITION

Rare Bird Books supports copyright. Copyright fuels creativity, encourages diverse voices, promotes free speech, and creates a vibrant culture. Thank you for buying an authroized edition of this book and for complying with copyright laws by not reproducing, scanning, or distributing any part of it in any form without permission. You are supporting writers and allowing Rare Bird Books to continue to publish books for readers to enjoy and appreciate.

All rights reserved, including the right to reproduce this book
or portions thereof in any form whatsoever, including
but not limited to print, audio, and electronic.

For more information, address:
Rare Bird Books Subsidiary Rights Department
6044 North Figueroa Street
Los Angeles, CA 90042

Excerpts from the novel appeared in *The Brooklyn Rail*,
Manhattan Magazine, and *Forever Magazine*.

Set in Minion
Printed in the United States

10 9 8 7 6 5 4 3 2 1

Library of Congress Cataloging-in-Publication Data available upon request

To Mom

PART 1

1

The Other Man

Celia and I had just returned from a weekend away at an apartment owned by my uncle, a small place on the beach in Westhampton abutting the sand and dunes with a clear view straight to the ocean. For three days we had been as happy as two people could be together: the sex, the wine, the fine foods, the long beach walks, the meaningful conversation. That it would still lead back to *this*—no, no, I couldn't do it anymore.

"Celia, this has to end. I've been up against it for over a year. I'm done."

"Paul, please," she said.

"Get a divorce—*get it* and I'll spend my whole life with you. Until then, I won't see you again. Don't call me. I don't want to hear from you. I mean it."

We had had many such conversations, especially of late, and yet I had never given Celia the ultimatum. But standing on a Brooklyn corner and delivering her back to her husband once again now, the awful ritual of watching the woman I loved walk from one life into the other, back and forth, up and down, here and gone, it all had to stop this very minute.

"Paul," she said. "We need to talk. I have to tell you something important."

"No, I'm sorry. No more talking. Goodbye."

Celia turned away first, a tall, long, brown-haired figure in a white slip hurrying inside a three-story building covered in black soot and graffiti. I watched her, staring long after she'd disappeared. A large truck motoring down the warehouse-flanked avenue brought me back to myself.

Why—*why* was Celia still married to Graham? They had *opened* their marriage to save it, but the result had only been more strain and confusion, more frustration and sadness. Moreover, she and Graham no longer wanted the same lives. Celia had come to New York to pursue a life of painting, something she had envisioned for herself going back to the age of twelve while growing up in Knoxville, Tennessee, whereas Graham hadn't been so sure about moving to New York in the first place and often talked of returning home to Atlanta and the slow, quiet pace of the South. Since meeting eight years ago at the University of Georgia and marrying young, Celia had always encouraged Graham to live as he must. He was a woodworker by trade and if sitting around and whittling a stick all day was his desire, then so be it. But what Celia really wanted in her husband was a partner-in-crime, a coconspirator.

Though we were both just over six feet tall and slim, Graham had a clear British ancestry, with his straight long brown hair and blue eyes, while my Jewish lineage was equally apparent in my curly black hair, dark eyebrows, etcetera. Graham wore vintage suits with kerchiefs neatly folded in the breast pockets and suspenders and on occasion a deerstalker hat, the same as Sherlock Holmes. Graham also took twice as long as Celia to dress. She would be late to a dinner party because Graham couldn't decide on which pair of socks went best with an outfit. Celia clearly preferred being with a man who could throw on pants and a button down and leave the apartment in under five minutes. More to the point, I was a born and raised New Yorker with a strong sense of impatience, and Celia was in New York now. There was no time for waiting around, she had places to be.

One hour later Celia called me and said she was coming straight to my apartment on the Upper West Side. We had to talk; I had no choice in the matter, she had something very important to say. Desperate and hurting yet still knowing she wouldn't tell me anything I hoped to hear, I agreed. Also, I began to remove all traces of her from my home. Photos of Celia on the refrigerator and by the bed, love letters in the desk drawer, a lock of her brown hair on the mantle and beside it the small oil painting she had made for me of my hero, the architect, Stanford White—I threw it all in a box, which I shoved to the back of a closet. She might notice the change upon arriving here; I could drive home the message that I would be moving on from her. Because any minute now, Celia would walk in and say it again: *I can never leave Graham. We have a whole life together. Our mothers and fathers are so close, our brothers and sisters bonded. And what would they say? And what would our friends say? And how could Graham and I not be together? I don't see how it's possible. I love you but I can't. I need you but I won't.*

And then, *I'm sorry.*

And also, *I'm sorry. I'm sorry.*

The downstairs buzzer had barely finished its ring and I was on my feet, undoing the lock at the door, descending the five flights of stairs—going down, down, down, past my neighbors and the noise of a baby crying and the drone of a vacuum cleaner running along carpet. And now Celia and I were about to have our final words. Yes, this was it: the end. And would I ever love again? But who? And did I have no choice in any of this? No—no choice in all the loneliness and despair that lay ahead.

I opened the heavy wooden door with its cold brass handle and Celia lunged into my arms.

"Okay, Paul," she said. "Okay."

"Okay, *what?*"

"Okay, I'll do it. I'll leave Graham."

"What? *Really?* You'll leave him?"

"Yes."

"Oh, Celia," I said, "I love you."

"I love you, too, Paul. We have to do this."

"We do, *we do*. We have to be together."

"Yes, we do. But the thing is, Paul…you see, Paul…the reason is, Paul…"

"Come in, Celia. Come in."

Had it started raining outside? Her skin was damp in my hands, her face lightly glistening. I led her to the foot of my bed, brought her a towel, a glass of ice-cold water. In the same white slip she'd had on when I dropped her at her apartment some two hours ago, with her lovely bare shoulders flushed with color and heat, she lay back on my bed, her head on the pillow. I collapsed beside her. We stared into one another's eyes. We held hands. Our knees knocked together, feet touching, and the late-afternoon April light shone through the nearby window. Her breathing had grown heavy. She seemed like she might be at the edge of losing it altogether, but I had never seen her forfeit control of herself like that. She never broke down, never gave into her anxieties, never even raised her voice or spoke a word that had to be taken back—and she wouldn't do any of those things now. Instead, she tightened her grip on my hand, squeezing harder and harder. She tipped her forehead forward an inch so that it leaned against my brow. Her nose touched my nose. It occurred to me that I should unpack that box of all things Celia, at least the photos, less she noticed. Celia would take seriously the fact that I had eliminated her image from my home in such short time. She wouldn't understand that I had done it to save myself from pain. Maybe when she got up to use the bathroom, yes, that would be the time for it.

"I'm pregnant," said Celia.

That box was in the closet, wasn't it? I *had* put it away. It wasn't sitting out for her to see, was it? "You're pregnant?" I said.

"Yes, Paul."

"You're *pregnant?*"

"Yes, Paul. Yes."

"Celia...oh, Celia...this...*this* is the greatest news ever!"

"Shhhh. Don't talk, please, Paul. Just hold me, please. Please, just hold me."

I swept Celia up in my arms, her back against me, my face in her neck. Could I hear sniffles? Was her body trembling? Was she crying now? I was about to ask her, but her grip on my hand became so strong I thought she would break my fingers off. Our knees lifted together into the shape of a seven and she drew my arms even tighter around her midsection, rolling herself up inside me.

2
Break the Bed

"Harder, harder, harder, harder—"

"Any harder, I'll break the bed, Paul."

"Good, break the bed."

"No, no, we can't break it," said Celia, rising and falling in the dark bedroom. "Graham, he built this bed. It took him over a year. I love this bed."

We didn't typically talk while having sex. Occasionally a dirty word or two would slip out, but certainly nothing about our relationship. I kissed Celia on the face, the forehead. And as long as we were on this constructive, communicative path, I said, "Well, what about this apartment?"

"What *about* the apartment?"

"I worry that we shouldn't be here, that it's not good for us."

"Do you think?"

"Sometimes I do, yes."

Graham had moved out two months ago. The paperwork on the divorce had just been filed, and now that Celia and I were going to start a family, we would be well-served with a fresh start. The classic Bushwick Avenue railroad was cheap, though, and we couldn't afford a better place. Bearing all of that in mind, panting, gasping, I took Celia's backside in both hands and said, "I got rid of *my* apartment because it was too small for us, especially considering a little boy is on the way. But now, over here, we've got other problems."

Graham. His influences, his flourishes, his designs, and still all his things, were everywhere. The shoe rack, the coat stand, the two-person bench at the front door, the dining table, the bookcase in the bedroom *and* the one in the studio—he hadn't taken any of it. He claimed not to have the room at the new place. But I sensed something else was up here: for instance, the inability to let go, to move on, to complete the transition from life with Graham to life with me.

"Graham built all these pieces with his mind and heart on his future with *you*."

"He did. That's true."

"It's a lot to be around."

"I understand. But these things are precious to me."

The lovemaking stopped. We lay in silence, Celia's head resting on my chest, her breathing steady. I waited for her to say something about the apartment or about Graham or about how our child, who we were so eager to welcome into the world, deserved a home with a less complex history. But Celia didn't speak, not a word.

Finally, I said, "Look, I understand that it's not as if you and I are going to get all new kitchenware just because every time I use a pot or pan or a fork or knife, I think of how you and Graham acquired these things in the process of building a life together. That would be ridiculous."

"That's right, it would be."

"And then no matter what measures you take, you can't do away with a person's past. Inevitably, it follows. A new coat stand wouldn't change this fact."

"It really wouldn't."

"*And* I'm sorry—I don't mean to push you. You're carrying our child."

"It's okay. He's doing well. He's being very good to me—no morning sickness, no fatigue. I'm very lucky."

To hear her speak this way about the baby growing inside her—*our baby*—there was nothing better. *Nothing*. Neither one of us had wavered at the news of the pregnancy. Both nearing thirty and wanting children and being in love, we were thrilled. Sure, Graham's presence—his figurative shadow cast by each bit of light and his literal camping gear collecting dust beneath the bed—was not ideal, but then a person couldn't have *everything* his way.

"I know I'm better off being realistic and acting rationally."

"Well, let's definitely strive for that," said Celia, climbing back on top of me. "Now *shhh*." She put a finger over my lips. "You talk too much, baby. No more talking, please."

The lovemaking continued then, but I couldn't help but notice out the corner of my eye a beautiful wooden chest that Graham had built. About four feet across, two feet wide, one foot deep, metal hinges, simple, utilitarian, Graham used to store his clothes inside of it—and now I was the one storing *my* clothes there. Each morning I flipped open the chest door and took out a pair of socks or a T-shirt, and a tinge of some unhappiness would rise inside me. The feeling was so brief, it seemed to last just the length of time that the chest door was open. The instant I shut it—*pffft!* gone—and I wouldn't think about any of it again. That is until the following day, when I would have to take out a new change of clothes.

With Celia's body heavy on me now, her one hand on my face and the other in my hair, her lips kissing my shoulder, I made a note to myself: Get rid of the chest, put it on the street, keep your clothes someplace else. Do it soon. Plenty of changes to make around the home—*our* home.

3
Making It

"Where did you come from, young lady? You're a master."

In the living room of a Fifth Avenue apartment with a view straight down into the Metropolitan Museum of Art, the seventy-something-year-old Broadway producer who had commissioned Celia to paint her three blonde granddaughters kneeled before the large canvas. I had carried the painting here on the subway from Williamsburg—four months pregnant, Celia wasn't supposed to lift heavy objects—and now I stood in the corner of the sprawling room, sipping a club soda.

"How do you even do this? Where does this ability come from? It's just marvelous, Celia. I could cry."

Celia, always measured, proffered a smile with just the right side of her face. "Your grandchildren make for good subjects."

"No, *you're* brilliant," said the producer in her red pants suit, gold jewelry on her fingers and ears and around her neck. "This painting could hang in the halls of the Met."

Celia, barely showing in black velvet pants and a yellow sweater, commanded the attention back to the painting, pointing out moments she particularly liked—the long curly hair of the youngest granddaughter, the folded hands of the eldest. She had placed three daisies in the top right corner of the painting. These flowers didn't live in a vase but seemed to float in the air. It was a wonderful decision, we all agreed.

"It's just magical. I could look at this painting forever."

"Good news—it's yours now and you can," said Celia.

Out on Fifth Avenue afterward, Celia folded a check for $7,000, the second half of her $14,000 fee, and placed it in her wallet. Celia was the only person I knew who could make her entire living off her art. While I was often impressed by this, Celia was not, for her income was entirely made up of commissioned portraits and while the sheer beauty of these paintings was overwhelming, it wasn't the kind of beauty that caught the attention of galleries. Celia's own *un-commissioned* work—realistic figurative oil paintings of friends in conversation, by and large—were unfashionable. No one would show them. She could hardly get a gallerist to visit her studio. Video and performance art, textiles and installations, were the focus of the industry. Painting was not just out-of-fashion but dead.

Walking alongside Central Park, I said that it would just never make sense to me. She was too talented. No one would say otherwise.

"Like anything, it's all about the trends."

"One day the trends will change and you'll be a star. I know it."

"We'll see. Pregnancy, motherhood—it's all going to slow me down for a bit."

"Yes. But I'll help you through it and we'll get you going again. Until then, it's amazing to have people react to your paintings with such joy and appreciation."

"I like it, too," said Celia. "And to be clear, I'm not complaining. I love making portraits. I have nothing but respect for the history and the work of the great portrait painters." Cassatt and Whistler were of particular importance to her. "But with your column, for instance, you get to speak directly to people about the things you care about. You have a voice. That's all I'm saying, Paul—I want that, too."

"Column" was a generous term for a newsletter received by some 10,000 people every week via email and paid for by the real estate activist, Cal Lowenstein. I couldn't say how many of the recipients actually opened the email and read it. I wouldn't dare look at the analytics. But then the gig paid for rent each month and I loved the work.

"You get to speak about the things that are important to you, Paul."

"I suppose that's worth something."

"It's worth a lot. I want that, too."

"You'll get there. I know it will happen."

Celia threw her hands in the air. She hated this subject. Twenty-nine years old, she had been in New York five years and having this discussion all along: with peers, with friends, with Graham, and now with me. She was tired of it.

"Thank you, Paul. Please, let's talk about anything else."

The Cursed Corners of New York City, a Newsletter

Over the past years in New York City, we have witnessed closures of stores, restaurants, movie theaters—businesses of all kinds—on a scale that most have not seen in their lifetimes. The identity of the city is shifting quickly, dramatically, and the empty storefronts piling up on nearly every block throughout the five boroughs is very much at the center of this change. A crisis of this magnitude requires our immediate attention. By considering the phenomenon of the cursed corner—those corner commercial spaces that cycle through one tenant after another and often spend long periods vacant—this newsletter aspires to open eyes and awaken minds to the very factors at the forefront of the city's empty commercial spaces. At the heart of this mission is a deep love of New York as well as a fear that we must act at once to get our storefronts occupied or else suffer great, perhaps irreversible, consequences to our neighborhoods.

The Beekman Tower

A curse looms at the Beekman Tower at the corner of 49th and First Avenue. The Deco gem, built between 1927-1928, and originally called the Panhellenic, was as aspirational in its vision as the tower's design itself suggests: a hotel and club offering inexpensive housing to women entering the workforce following the end of WWI. Conceived of and improbably realized in its totality by Emily Eaton Hepburn, five years before construction even began, a Panhellenic House Association was formed, incorporating so that funds could be raised and stock in the future property offered. Sororities across the country all *contributed to the fundraising efforts—it was in many ways a door-to-door operation—and eventually two mortgages were secured from Met Life together totaling $1.2 million. The Panhellenic opened in October 1928 and was an immediate sensation, as well as the only hotel in New York owned and operated by women. In 1932, the building's interior was changed to accommodate male guests and soon after renamed the Beekman Towers. The Beekman remained a sorority hub until it was sold by the Panhellenic House Association to the Lyden Realty Corporation in 1964. That transaction, naturally, gave birth to the curse. Since then, the building has changed hands many times, most recently between Silverstein Properties (World Trade Center) and a company called Reside by Adoba. From inspired beginnings!*

The Breuer Building

What circumstances create a cursed corner? In almost all cases, an original tenant has vacated a location and a new tenant has attempted to insert itself—and its vision or perhaps lack of one—into that very space.

Now say hello to one of New York City's newest cursed corners. Some would say it has always been cursed. But when the Whitney Museum vacated its longtime home and moved downtown, it left behind a building with a very difficult premise. In just a blip the Met Breuer is on its way out and the Frick is temporarily storing its collection there during a renovation. And then what? You can already sense what is a growing identity crisis for a building that dares any new tenant to try and occupy it. Curse, you are cruel.

The South Street Seaport

The South Street Seaport is cursed, not on a corner-by-corner basis, but the whole area collectively. Nowhere does the curse become more expressed than at Pier 17, which has recently cut a ribbon on its third demolish-and-do-over shopping mall in my lifetime. The pitch this time around to would-be Seaport shoppers is more desperate than ever. Now three celebrity chefs are promising a "New Concept." The term "New Concept" gives me the chills and reeks of the curse, a smell far more terrible than that of the fish stalls that once populated the area, a nasty stench. I suspect the new building will be gone in the next fifteen years, replaced by the latest model. How unfortunate. How cursed.

4

The Support of His Family

I was off to meet my mother this morning, a long-overdue catchup twice postponed by her. Resultantly, I hadn't yet told her she was going to be a grandmother. But I would bring her up to date on everything now. I would try, anyhow.

My mother was living on Madison Avenue in the Carlyle Hotel, a resident for just over ten years, having moved in after I went off to college. Despite the history of the building, its luxury and prestige, I had always found it strange that she should call a hotel her home, but my mother said the accommodations worked well for her. Her entire life revolved around the hotel. She knew the staff, the bellhops, the housekeepers, the elevator attendant—these were the people she spoke to, the ones whose lives she put effort into knowing. She made herself available to them, invited them into her apartment. I had heard it straight from their mouths: any one of them would see me with my mother in the lobby and tell me how wonderful she was, the best listener, the *very* best. She had never been that kind of mother to me. In truth, I had had to spend my entire youth listening to *her* every woe. So yes, when the elevator attendant patted me on the shoulder and told me how wonderful it was to have my mother to talk to, the most resourceful advisor he had ever known, it did hurt, if only a little.

I'd forgotten to have my mother meet me upstairs in her apartment today. Now, making her way through the lobby, any attention she might have shown me was already shifted into greeting not only every member of the hotel staff but also a few guests she clearly didn't know at all. She was so cheerful, my mother, smiling at everyone. And she looked wonderful in a flowing gown, all gold: golden hair, golden nails and makeup, and jewelry, of which there was plenty. A small woman, she carried herself with her elbows drawn back at the sides, hands held up near her shoulders as if she were floating on air. Her eyes were big and blue but discerning, never lost. At last, they fell to me, and I smiled at her. I shouldn't be angry with her, I thought. What more could a person want for his mother at her late age but to have a place, to have people, to feel comfortable being herself.

"How are you, Paul?"

"Mom."

The waiter brought us to our table and told my mother how wonderful it was to see her. He was a handsome, dark-haired man. He could be my mother's lover for all I knew. They clearly had a bond and a language of their own.

"Can I get a cup of coffee, sir?"

"His name is Fred," said my mother.

"Can I get a cup of coffee, *Fred?*"

Fred signaled that he would be back in a moment. But before he walked away, another waiter, Don, brought my mother a cup of chamomile tea and kissed her on the cheek and said good morning to her. Don was a few years Fred's senior, firmly in middle-age, small and light-eyed and buzzing. He assured my mother that a few extra lemon wedges were there for her on the saucer. My mother spent the next few minutes squeezing these lemon wedges one by one into her tea. Meanwhile, she and I talked about life, mostly hers, but mine as well. My mother was once a very busy person, running her own apparel line—her own parents had been in the luggage business—and presumably raising a child as well. She had been in constant motion then. But she seemed perfectly comfortable doing less of everything while this hotel created an impression of busyness around her. And then she had her relationships here. This was what I had to hear about now: how she spent so much time talking with the hotel staff, the piano player at Bemelmans, the guests.

"How's that job of yours, the one about the *unusual* corners? Did you get a new one yet?"

"No, Mom. I'm very happy with my job."

"Hmm. Not too happy, I hope. I see your father's influence in this."

My father was an architect and had taught me about *looking*, about pulling back the layers of a building and finding the story within the structure. As a child, he would walk me around the city for hours and hours, discussing the significance of this detail or why that building was constructed in such and such a way, why one material was used instead of another, and then how almost nothing I saw before me would be around in a century or two, that everything fell apart or went away in time, that permanence was an illusion—albeit one perpetuated by every architect alive or dead—where impermanence was truth. He never stayed in one place for long, my father. My mother said that they had divorced after only a few years together because he refused to ever come home. He could be anywhere in the world right now, at work on a project. Dubai, Stockholm, Sao Paolo, Miami, Shanghai. We almost never spoke, which secretly delighted my mother who once called my newsletter a grand attempt at reaching him. This was probably why she didn't like the job, but then she didn't approve of much else in my life either, so it was hard to know for certain.

"And what about that girlfriend of yours, Celia? Is she still married?"

"No, Mom, that's all been resolved."

"You're sure?"

I said, "I was just about to tell you that Celia is—"

"I need more lemon."

My mother stood from her seat and went to find Don or Fred or whomever else was out there. Returning with a plate of lemon wedges, she said, "My room is being cleaned now. I don't let them wash the bedding every day. It's not necessary, and it's wasteful. But some people do, and that's their prerogative. I don't judge. I just don't think a person's sheets and pillowcases have to be laundered on a daily basis. The man who does the laundry, Orlando, is just a lovely person. Some nights after he gets off I like to go on walks with him, if the weather is right."

"I'm glad you have companionship, Mom."

"Oh, I have more than companionship. I have *ties*. Don, more lemon, please."

"Mom, do you really need more lemon? Don't you think you have enough?"

"Excuse me," she said. "I know how much lemon I need, thank you very much. What's got into you?"

"Nothing," I said.

Don, a sprig of a man with short white hair, set down a small plate of lemon wedges. My mother took one between thumb and forefinger and held it there, thinking. Seconds passed.

"Mom, I have to tell you, Celia—"

"So she got the divorce?"

"Yes, yes, that's done. She got it. But there's more—there's much more. You're going to be a grandmother. Celia, she's pregnant."

"What?" My mother looked everywhere but at me and then began to rise from her seat. "I can't believe this. What is this? What are you saying? Celia's pregnant!"

"Yes, Mom." I was about to apologize but stopped myself. I went to my mother instead, drew her by the arm, a frailer arm than I remembered her having.

She said, "But isn't she still married to the other one?"

"No, I'm telling you, they're divorced. It's done."

"And you're sure it's your baby?"

"Yes! It's my baby."

"You're sure?"

"Yes, Mom!"

"Well, but don't you want to wait a moment to start a family and see if the relationship *sticks?*"

"I love her, Mom. We *want* to have a baby together. We want to start a family. What more is there to say?"

"Oh lord, Paul, there is much, *much* more to say."

"Mom—"

"Don, please," my mother suddenly screamed, "more lemon!"

5

Down South

Celia was eager to get down to Knoxville to see her family before she was too pregnant to fly. Though her mother and stepfather had moved away, first to Hawaii and then Indiana to pursue better-paying jobs, Celia's father and his wife were still living in her hometown. The relative ease of the first trimester had given way to more months of good health. If you asked Celia how she was feeling, she would tell you she was absolutely fine.

It was the first question put to her by her father, D.W. He had arrived at the Knoxville airport thirty minutes late to pick us up, unsurprisingly, as it were. Like his accent, his life had a kind of drawl to it, a lag. His height seemed to have something to do with this. It took effort to lift those large feet and extend his long legs and carry forward his upper bulk. You wouldn't tell a giant to hurry up for the obvious reason that he might use his strength on you, but also because he wouldn't be able to go any faster if he tried. D.W. called his daughter Nippers, as in, "How was the flight, Nippers?" and spoke with a gentleness that could almost be mistaken for sadness. He carried his daughter's suitcase, despite the handle and wheels available to him, lumbering through the uncrowded baggage claim, a bit off-kilter and about six feet ahead of us.

He was silent in the white Jeep Cherokee, riding back to the house. Celia tried to make small talk: she inquired about Lily, D.W.'s wife of some ten years, tried to find out how her school year was going—she taught fourth grade— and the latest on Lily's sons. D.W. answered, though never with more than three words. I sat in the back of the car not saying much myself. I had already met D.W. and Lily during a trip to Knoxville some eight months back. If our past visit had told me anything, it was that D.W. was open-minded and could accept that his then married daughter was in an open relationship and seeing other people. That is, in his quiet style, he had treated me with kindness and decency. I also learned that he would offer me a very tall glass of whiskey and ice the moment we came in the door and that he would keep my glass full for the remainder of the trip, and for that I was grateful.

But then shortly after arriving at his home, with Celia and I having put our suitcases down and said hello to Lily and settled onto the patio overlooking the bean-shaped swimming pool, D.W. handed me a glass of tepid water with a single ice cube and then lowered himself onto a folding chair that nearly collapsed beneath his weight. Taking a moment to find his voice, he finally said, "Listen here, son— you listening?—you are going to marry my Celia, all right? You hearing me?"

I didn't doubt that I had heard him correctly. The severity of his tone assured me that I had understood him, too. Celia sat silently in a chair near the pool's edge, her big brown eyes downcast and her painter's hands folded on the curvature of her stomach. Lily, a redheaded daughter of Knoxville, a tall, ex-beauty contestant, set a tray of salty snacks down onto a picnic table and said, "Now, D.W., please," but nothing more.

In the folding chair beside D.W., I took in a mouthful of the lukewarm water, holding it at the back of my throat before swallowing. "Sir," I said, "I appreciate where you're coming from—"

"*What?* You appreciate it, son?"

"Yes, but I don't know if Celia and I will get married. I'm sorry, but—"

"Oh, no, no—you're not hearing me, Paul. *You* are not hearing me."

"And, right, yes, well, I mean, Celia and I have discussed marrying and I just can't say with any confidence that it's where she and I are heading and—"

"Young man, you are *not* hearing me."

"Yes, I know, but here's the thing, sir, because I want to spend my whole life with your daughter and I want to be buried in the plot directly next to hers and I know that one hundred and ten percent, and you have my word and I'd write it for you in blood."

"*Paul!* Do you have a hearing problem? Answer me. Do you? Can you not hear, son?"

"No, sir. I do not have a hearing problem."

"Are you sure? Have you had your hearing checked? Have you? Have you been to a doctor?"

"I have not, sir."

"Well, you might want to schedule an appointment." D.W.'s gaze was set forward toward the cool clear sky above. Exhaling, tense and laboring, he said, "Now if I have to drag your ass to the chapel, son, I will drag your ass to the chapel."

"Sir, I don't—"

"Son, I will put you in that flippin' car out front and I will haul your ass up the drive and down the road to that chapel. Do you hear me?"

"Yes, sir. I think I do, but—"

"Because you are marrying my daughter."

"Okay. Thank you, yes."

"You *are* marrying her."

"Yep. Yes. Yes, I am."

D.W. stood, his giant mass unfolding part by part until it assumed a towering presence over me. His right eye twitched, his dimpled chin held drops of sweat. I didn't know if he would pick me up next and throw me into the swimming pool, where an orange Volunteers raft floated on the surface of the water. D.W. himself seemed unsure what to do now, his body perhaps in conflict with itself, as if his head and limbs could not agree on a direction. I braced, then I heard D.W. huff and all of a sudden he was marching back into the house.

Lily flashed us a concerned look and then followed after him.

Once the sliding glass door had closed behind her, I rose from my seat, and said, "Holy fucking hell."

"You did great, baby."

"Great? You think so?"

"He loves me so much. Can you blame him? It really was very sweet of him."

"I mean, sure, okay, but is he going to fucking kill me?"

"Daddy? No."

The color in Celia's cheeks was full, ruddy. Her eyes gleamed with pride.

I lowered to my knees, taking her hands. I said, "You know I do want to spend my whole life with you and be buried next to you? You know that, don't you? I meant that."

"You promise?"

"Absolutely—yes, I promise."

"Should we get married then?"

"I don't know. Maybe we should," I said, kissing Celia's pregnant stomach. "We could."

"I just don't know what I think of marriage anymore."

"I understand. But maybe our kid will be happier if his parents are married."

"That could be."

"Maybe we do get married. Maybe I'm going to put a large rock on your finger."

"You will not."

"Maybe I will—a big rock for the whole village to see."

"You better not," said Celia, squeezing me close to her. "Just tell me you love me and that you always will."

"I love you and I always will," I said.

"You promise me, Paul?"

"I do. I promise, I promise," I said. "Now let's go find a hotel."

6
Nursey Rhymes

Graham had moved nearby into an old warehouse on Driggs in Williamsburg, a sprawling industrial space that he shared with friends. Offered a bedroom there, he had opted for a large closet. He slept on a wooden plank and used a two-by-four in place of a pillow. In Graham's estimation, denying himself these basic comforts was a nod to the order of the monks whom he so greatly admired. Was he upset about his wife leaving him? How about her carrying another man's child? He had never said anything about it directly to Celia, nor had he addressed me on the matter. But after moving out of the apartment, he had ridden a bicycle from New York to Seattle, sleeping in ditches along the side of the road. On the journey, he lost nearly a third of his already negligible body weight. He had briefly planned to move to Micronesia, an island located somewhere between Hawaii and the Philippines, which sounded both made up and like a cry for help. His relocation had been contingent on a job offer, one that had ultimately been rescinded, and so instead of being employed on a remote island on the other side of the world he was now working for a woodworker right here in Brooklyn.

He had promised Celia that he would do some work around the apartment before our child was born, attend to some of the long-standing problems that predated my arrival: the broken lock on the bathroom window, a doorknob that had continued to fall off, a shim-job on an off-balanced bookcase, a leak under the kitchen sink, a lamp that had to be rewired, a chair leg that needed reinforcement. Celia and I left the apartment for a couple of hours so that he could come over and do the work one Saturday shortly before her due date and when we returned what we discovered was not only a fixed bathroom window and a new doorknob and a shimmed bookcase, but an entire nursery custom-built by Graham.

"This is fucking insane," I said.

"I know, look at the crib, it's fit for a prince," said Celia, holding the hump of her stomach in the crook of her arm.

The crib was exquisite, made of a cocoa-colored wood. Next to the crib were cubbies, twelve-squares, four across and three levels high, a handsome piece of furniture on which Graham had placed a brand-new light up globe. There was a changing table with a built-in drawer, its knob inlaid with mother-of-pearl. Who knew how many hours of work he had put into building these pieces—ten, fifteen, maybe twenty or more? Celia and I drew our hands up and down the furniture in a state of utter disbelief. Graham had said nothing to prepare us for *this*, not a word. There was a card in which Graham explained how excited he was for the birth of our child and how this nusery was an expression of those feelings.

"Do you think we should say something, Celia?"
"Like what?"
"Like: *seek help*."
"That's not funny, Paul."
"I agree. None of this is funny."
"Come on, he's done such great work. Who could argue with that?"
"I could. I could argue with all of it."
"But you won't. Now stop, *please*."

Celia insisted on having Graham over the following night so that we could toast to his efforts with a few rounds of Fernet, his favorite spirit. Graham arrived wearing the Sherlock Holmes hat and carrying a pipe he didn't smoke but merely held while he went on for more than forty minutes about the inspiration for the nursery: the furniture in a monastery that he and Celia had visited in Tuscany in their early twenties. We hadn't even gotten to the Fernet nor the hors d'oeuvres Celia had picked up earlier in the day. I was about to propose we do so, but then Graham took some kind of butter cookie out of the pocket of his suit jacket and began nibbling on it. Crumbs fell on his collar and on the floor. He spoke with his mouth full.

"I'm so sorry, Paul," he said, interrupting himself mid-thought. "I've been talking the whole time, haven't I?"

Celia glared at me, arms crossed.

I held up my hands, shook my head. "No, no, carry on. I'm interested in all of it."

"You're sure?" said Graham.

"Absolutely."

Graham smiled. Then he began to describe how monks in medieval times would have kept their prayer books on a piece of furniture that almost exactly resembled the new changing table, then about how he had driven to a special lumber yard four hours away in Pennsylvania where a particular strain of mahogany could be had and not for cheap, and then there was at least another half hour of Graham talking about the two all-nighters he had pulled so that he could sneak into a friend's workshop in the off-hours and use its high-end machinery (saws, sanders). I sat there, drinking steadily, though I did not like Fernet, and at some point it occurred to me that I was very drunk and also that this apartment was bursting with Graham's furniture and that it couldn't hold any more of it and that I had to push back.

"Excuse me a moment, everyone."

Celia and Graham didn't seem to notice me stand and go into the bedroom. In the corner was the chest built by Graham, which I emptied onto the floor—socks, underwear, sweatpants, T-shirts. The chest was ever-slightly larger than I imagined, cumbersome in my arms and pinching at the skin. On seeing me enter the kitchen now, Graham and Celia both rose from their seats.

"Graham," I said, "I'm putting this at the door. Take it with you tonight when you leave."

"Oh, no, no," said Graham, holding the pipe out toward me, his brow creased under the brim of the Sherlock hat. "That's yours, Paul."

"No, no, no, no, it's yours. You're *taking* it."

"He wants you to have it," said Celia. She'd tied back her hair tonight with a red ribbon, her unobstructed eyes big, clear, purposeful.

I placed the chest at the door. "It's a great piece, Graham. Gorgeous, truly. You do such good work. But take it with you tonight. I have a new chest coming."

"You ordered a new chest?" said Celia.

"No, not yet. But soon, tomorrow. Graham, you'll take the chest. It's your chest. Take the chest."

"Paul, I want you to have that chest."

"No. It's yours. Take it with you, please, for the love of God!"

We stood in silence around the untouched hors d'oeuvres. I could feel Celia staring at me, the intensity of her look. Heat moved through my cheeks, my arms and hands, down to my feet.

"It's a great chest, Graham, but I don't want it. Take it with you tonight. Okay?"

"Okay," said Graham.

"Thank you."

Graham put his hand on my shoulder now, leaning in close to me. "If you want, Paul…if you don't like the chest, I could make you a new one. Would that be better? I'm happy to make one for you if you like. It wouldn't be a problem. No, it would be my pleasure. I mean it."

7

Blizzards & Births

Celia's contractions began during a blizzard on the night of December 28. In good weather the Natural Birthing Center in Upper Manhattan was a thirty-minute car ride from our apartment, but there was almost two feet of snow accumulated on the ground and who knew how our taxi driver would even navigate his car in these conditions. The black sedan was parked outside the apartment. The time was 4:02 a.m. Visibility was almost none. The traffic lights were all being tossed about like buoys in choppy water. Garbage bags tied to receptacles on street corners were turned inside out by the wind and blowing around as if lifted by angry spirits. In the backseat of the car, Celia's contractions were slowing down, and by the time we arrived at the birthing center they had stopped completely.

Inside, Celia and I were sent into a small room with a queen-sized bed and a standing lamp. What about Celia's contractions? The midwives explained that in the process of traveling from home they had receded, which was normal, we would simply have to wait for them to start up again. How long that would take was anyone's guess, but Celia and I were just so grateful to have made it here in the blizzard. One of the midwives said we ought to be, that a mother scheduled to deliver at the birthing center had been unable to get out of her apartment building, the front door barricaded by snow, and she had given birth at home in her apartment as the midwives had talked her husband through the steps of how to support her.

We were told to make ourselves comfortable. But just then, Celia cried out in pain. Her contractions were back. The next one came in less than three minutes. Celia was breathing heavily, her hands on the bulk of her stomach as if to slow the pressure caused by the oncoming baby. The contractions that followed were less than two minutes apart.

"This is the worst pain of my life. God, it hurts."

I went to find the midwives. Perhaps owing to my exhaustion or stress or both, I could hardly tell the four of them apart. Between forty and fifty years old, about five foot four inches tall, one hundred and ten pounds, blonde to strawberry-blonde hair, gaunt, pale, wiry, and in motion—no, they didn't stop moving from point to point to point around the birthing center, tending to responsibilities. One midwife in training was easy to tell apart because she had none of the skill or deliberateness of the other midwives. Her name was Lucy. She was glad to hear the contractions had intensified. She would check the heart rate of the baby. To do so, she would have to locate the whereabouts of the baby's heart with a fetal monitor. Lucy, light bleary eyes, tangled reddish-blonde hair, tentative, drew the device over Celia's pelvic area, searched and searched but found nothing.

"Sorry," said Lucy. "It's really hard to find the heartbeat. Don't worry. I'm not worried. It's there. I'll get it."

I was prepared to tear the fetal monitor out of Lucy's hand and pinpoint the heartbeat myself. Instead, Merry, the midwife who seemed to do everything around here—file the paperwork, answer the phones, vacuum the carpets, examine the expecting mothers and deliver their babies—came into the room and did it.

"There it is," said Merry, the transducer held directly beneath Celia's belly button. The heart rate was steady, strong. The thumping of the baby's heart was the most glorious sound. Merry, who wore a red bandana over her head of long blonde hair and a pencil behind her ear, said:

"How do you feel, Celia? Are you comfortable? You need anything?"

"No, I'm fine," said Celia.

But at the next moment, Celia's labor began to rapidly accelerate. Now Merry and Lucy were on either side of her, with two additional midwives present, and were telling Celia not to push yet. They would say when. Not yet, no. Wait. Wait. *Now*.

"Push!" they told Celia.

Celia, seated at a slight angle on the bed, knees up, legs open, gown hoisted just past her buttocks, pushed with all her might, teeth clenched, eyes tightly shut, face bright red. One, two, three, push. One, two, three, push. Celia let out a deep moan—and then the midwives instructed her to stop pushing. She had to wait. They would let her know when she could start pushing again. And now here it came, and they told her to *push*, with Celia engaging what appeared to be every muscle in her body from her toes up through her forehead. Merry was seated between Celia's splayed legs and she said she could see the baby's head. Could she? The head? Could it be that this would all be over soon, the baby born, and Celia holding our child in her arms?

Merry instructed Celia to keep doing exactly what she was doing and to not change a thing. Her gaze was steady. "You've got this, Celia. You're almost done."

"You're there," said Lucy, hovering at the foot of the bed.

The two additional midwives who had come into the room were rooting Celia on, clapping, applauding. "You're a superstar, Celia. You've got this."

"You're doing it, Celia. You're getting there."

"Celia," said Merry, "just a little bit more. Just a little bit more."

But the baby's head, though crowning, was proving too large to exit Celia. Perhaps the midwives could help her find a better angle at which to push the baby out. Merry proposed drawing Celia a bath—there was a large tub in the bathroom—and she could stand up in the hot water and gravity would do something to assist in the process and Celia would be able to engage different muscles and push even harder. Celia agreed. It sounded promising. It looked so, too. Celia, stooped in the bath, her feet a good distance apart, left hand holding onto a metal bar, appeared primed to birth the baby. Merry asked her to push and Celia gave it her all, moaning deeply.

"Push! Push, Celia!" said Merry.

"Come on, Celia. You can do it. Push!" cried Lucy, as did the other midwives.

But with the next push, still nothing.

Celia flashed a dispirited look, one that brought a somberness to all the midwives.

"The baby's not coming out," she said. "I think his head is too large to get through. I've never been in so much pain in my life. Should we go to the hospital?"

"No. Not yet," said Merry. "Let's get you back in the bed, Celia, take vitals, and do a little more pushing. If you can have the baby here, that'll be for the best. Let's just give it one more try."

"I don't know how much more I can do," said Celia.

"Okay," said Merry. "I know. I know. Birthing a child is serious work. You've got this, though. You can do this."

A minute later, Celia was in the bed, and Merry, checking the baby's heart rate, noted that it had become slower.

Celia seemed to gather all her strength, repositioning herself at a slight angle. Her hands clutched the sheets, her toes curled. The midwives were urging her on, as was I, seated directly behind her. Merry said that she would count to three and then Celia should push. Here it came, this was it, the child would be born here and now, yes.

"Ready, Celia? Okay, here we go," said Merry. Her tone was stern. This was an order to push out her baby. "One, two, three!"

Celia began to push with her whole being. She released a sound that was part war cry, part plea for mercy. The baby's head was touchable, ready to emerge. And yet the head could not fit through, and there was nothing Celia could do now to change this fact. No amount of pushing would help.

An ambulance was called. The nearest hospital, Columbia Presbyterian, was about fifteen blocks away, but the streets were snow locked. The 911 dispatch wasn't willing to promise that an ambulance would even be able to make it to the address of the birthing center.

"Is an ambulance coming or not?" I asked Merry.

"Yes, yes, an ambulance is coming...I think."

"We'll get you to the hospital," I told Celia. "Don't worry. Let's get you dressed."

"I can't put on pants," she said. The baby was fully descended, the head partially out, the pressure immense. "Everything inside me wants to keep pushing."

"Hold on, you will get to push so soon," I said. "We'll be at that hospital in no time and you'll get to push and then you'll be holding our baby."

"Pass me my coat. I'm just going to wrap myself in it. Then let's go wait outside." So many blood vessels in her eyes had burst. I wrapped Celia in her coat.

In the vestibule of the birthing center, Celia and I held hands, quiet, numb, waiting. Minutes passed, beneath the low light of a single bulb. How was the baby doing? What was its heart rate? Was it still alive? Would the ambulance make it here? And if not, would we carry Celia through the blizzard for nearly a mile? Perhaps that's just how it would have to happen. Maybe we would hitch a ride from one of the trucks plowing the streets.

An ambulance pulled up in front of the birthing center. Two EMTs emerged, one with a clipboard, one with a gurney. Celia, coat draped over her shoulders, in sweater and boots but no pants, lay down on the gurney. Merry, Lucy, and the two other midwives, out in the wind and snow, told her not to worry, she would be fine. She had done an incredible job. The baby would soon be out, they promised.

I hurried alongside the gurney, as the EMTs wheeled Celia into the back of the ambulance. When the doors slammed, Celia and I looked at one another, a long silent exchange that required no words at all. The ambulance pulled out, and we were on our way to the hospital. Celia and I held hands, feeling the road beneath the tires, this icy passage. Through two small windows at the back of the ambulance, I saw abandoned cars littered throughout the streets in deep snow. The wind outside sounded monstrous, as if it could tear off a side of the vehicle.

"We're two blocks from the hospital, Celia. We're about to get that baby into your arms."

"I know we are," she said.

"Good. Just hold on, just hold on."

The ambulance pulled up at the emergency room entrance and within seconds the EMTs had the gurney out and were wheeling Celia into the ER. There was no signing in, just a straight passage through the bright fluorescent-lit hospital corridor into an elevator up to a higher floor, and at last, into an operating room.

A man walked in, brown mustache, blue scrubs, white latex gloves, medical mask hung around his neck, and he introduced himself as Dr. Mark. He no doubt recognized the look of trauma on Celia's face. Three nurses moved efficiently about the room, following the doctor's orders. The device in

Dr. Mark's hand was called a vacuum but resembled a toilet plunger. Next thing, Dr. Mark brought the vacuum between Celia's legs and applied the suction-cup to the end of the baby's crowning head.

"Okay, Celia, I'm going to count to three and then say push. Okay?"

"Yes," she said, two hands clutching the railings of the operating table.

"One...two...three...*push!*"

Celia let out a scream, and the doctor proceeded to pull on the vacuum with what looked to me like all his strength. Then suddenly, the suction cup popped off the baby's head.

Pop!

I was sure our child was dead. Vitals of both mother and baby were taken. Celia, who was not on any pain drugs, did not even make a sound. Her eyes looked out straight ahead at the doctor, who was now applying the vacuum to the baby's head a second time.

"All right, Celia...one, two, three, okay?"

"Yes, yes. Okay."

Again, Celia cried out, and Dr. Mark pulled hard on the vacuum, and again:

Pop!

Silence from Celia, the nurses, too.

"Okay, so here's the story," said Dr. Mark, poised, calm. "I'm going to put this vacuum on your baby's head once again and you're going to push him out, and if it doesn't work, we'll have to do a C-section."

"Just get the baby out of me!" said Celia. "Do whatever you have to do! *Please!*"

I pressed my hand to Celia's shoulder. Vitals were taken again. The baby's heart rate was lowering. Same with Celia's. Dr. Mark brought the suction cup to the baby's head a third time.

"All right, Celia, I want you to push with all you've got. Give it one really, *really* hard push, and we'll get the baby out of you right now. Okay? You're going to do it. You'll do it right now. You're ready? Good, good. I know you're ready! On three."

"Okay," she said.

"One...two...three!"

And Celia began to scream and push, and Dr. Mark was pulling so hard on the vacuum, and suddenly—suddenly—there was a baby in Dr. Mark's hands, and he cried out:

"It's a healthy baby boy!"

Dr. Mark placed the wailing baby on Celia's breast.

At the sight of Celia and the newborn, I began to weep. "Look at him," I said to Celia. "Look at that baby."

"Oh my God, my baby," she said, breathless, panting. "My baby, my baby, it's my baby."

"Celia, Celia, look at that baby. Our baby. Dr. Mark, did you see that!"

"I did. I saw it. Congratulations to you both," he said. "You make a beautiful family."

"Oh, my baby," said Celia, stroking the nursing newborn's red, swollen face. Tears streamed from her eyes. She said, "Paul, my love, come here, come close, come all the way in."

I brought my cheek to her cheek. "Celia, my love, you did it, you did it, you did it."

"*We* did it," she whispered into my ear. "We're a family now."

PART 2

8

A New Life

We named him after our favorite country music star, Waylon Jennings. Waylon came home from the hospital on New Year's Eve, only minutes before the ball dropped, and I held him close to my chest with one hand and raised a champagne flute to Celia with the other:

"I love you so much. Happy New Year," I said.

Celia touched her glass to mine, kissed me on the lips—and I was happier than I could ever recall being.

Waylon was perfect, the perfect baby, and I knew now that my desire to start a family with Celia had been based on something real, something true and honest. The weeks ahead only furthered this belief, with the three of us together in the apartment throughout the day or else walking around the neighborhood with nothing to do. Thoughts of the world beyond our home faded away. My mind was so quiet. I had never known peace like this. Where was the stress and pain of being? Why wasn't I worried about my newsletter, my finances, my health? Where was the fear that had confronted me first thing in the morning upon opening my eyes every day of my life going back to childhood? Had it been defeated?

Wiped out by the arrival of a ten-pound baby boy? That seemed impossible, but it was exactly what had happened. This family, *my family*, was the cure.

Some three weeks after Waylon's birth, Cal Lowenstein, my employer, began to hound me for the next cursed corner. Celia reminded me that we still needed to eat and pay rent, and I was at once filled with joy and purpose, emboldened with a new expectation of myself. Why, yes, my job supported my family, and what a beautiful thing. But then I didn't like to be out of the apartment working, wanting instead to be home with Celia and Waylon, and so I would rush through my process, subway to a neighborhood, walk about for as few minutes as possible until a cursed corner was identified. So many cursed corners everywhere, so easy to find, but not all of them as interesting as the next, not all of them demanding a place in my newsletter. On some days it took longer to find the kinds of corners that really moved my heart. But even when I did locate the very best cursed corners, I didn't exalt at my discovery as I once would have. No, I didn't care about anything but getting home to Celia and Waylon, and the moment I came in the door, swarmed by my two loves, I rejoiced.

When Waylon was three months old, I began to strap him in a carrier and take him with me to track down cursed corners. Everyone treated you a little bit better when you had a newborn attached to your chest. At delis and pharmacies, sure, but also at notoriously vicious government offices like the DMV and the post office, people now went out of their way for me, told me about the special deals or how adorable

Waylon was and how they just wanted to squeeze him. It was a special thing to behold all this humanity being brought forth by a baby.

One night, with Waylon asleep in his crib, Celia and I decided to play a game in which we would sit in bed and not talk about our baby. Nothing about an upcoming pediatrician appointment, nor long overdue visits to parents and grandparents to introduce Waylon, or whether the child was developing well and was happy, healthy. Nothing about Waylon's life at all. We would put those subjects down and discuss anything else. Like what? We thought for a minute, then another minute. Noses wrinkled, eyes searched the ceiling, lips fluttered. Apparently, we weren't up to this challenge.

"Should we just let ourselves talk about Waylon?"

"Probably," said Celia.

"Is something else wrong?"

"No, no. But actually it turns out they're having a birthday party for Graham just down the street. I want to pop over and say happy birthday."

"Oh—oh, okay," I said. "Of course. Go."

"You mean it?"

A moment later, Celia was changing out of her pajamas into a silver party dress. A sensible, straight forward matter, except that the moment Celia opened the front door to leave, I witnessed her body lighten with the taste of opportunity and she looked so happy, almost child-like, so giddy and high. She called out to me, "I'll tell Graham you say happy birthday," and then the door closed behind her.

Fixing myself a whiskey and sitting down on the bench by the front door, a bench built by Graham, yes, I had to contend with this vision of Celia departing, her flight, the takeoff, the immediate ascension and sense of utter joy that had accompanied it, and the meaning of *that*. Was something not being said? Was I not picking up on something vital? But then Celia came home just two hours later and first things first, she said, to me, "Come on, let's go look at Waylon."

The bathroom light shone through the apartment, guiding us to our son's room. In his crib, Waylon lay gently snoring with his thumb in his mouth.

"I love him so much," said Celia. We took each other's hands, staring down at our sleeping child. "Don't you wish he would stay like this forever?"

"Like this? *No.* I'd like him to be a little older so that we can really get into it. Not that I'm in any rush for him to grow up."

"For me it's so sad that he's already this big, that he'll never be a tiny little baby again. Sometimes I even miss being pregnant."

"You're drunk, aren't you?"

"Seriously, Paul, I do, I miss it. Maybe we should have another child. I'd like another. Why not just have a big family. We'll get married finally and have a big, *big* family."

"I want to have a big family with you, Celia."

"Let's do it then. I'm in love with our child. I've never known I could love something as much as I love Waylon. I just didn't know that there was love *like* this. And isn't it amazing? Isn't it, though? Yes, the love itself, but also that you can live your life for some thirty years and feel so much and feel it all so intensely and all the while be unable to imagine that there could be a feeling that's larger and more meaningful than any of the others you've ever had. Then you carry this life inside of you and birth it into the world and stare day after day into its eyes and feed and nurture it, and you begin to realize that this love for your baby is the biggest, most powerful of all the feelings, Paul. Do you understand what I'm saying? There's just nothing bigger than the feeling a mother has for her baby. Nothing. And it's like a drug. Our baby drugs me, drugs me with feelings of love for him."

I didn't care that I would have to be up again long before the sun was due to rise to tend to Waylon, or that the wind could be heard howling outside the window and that would mean having to do my job tomorrow in the freezing cold. In here, I had everything there was to have.

The following morning, to give Celia time to sleep, I took Waylon with me to find my next cursed corners. Slipping out the front door, I heard Celia call to me from the bed. She said, "Thank you for letting me rest a little longer. Thank you for taking care of me. Thank you for doing your job well. Hurry back to me. I love you."

2 Columbus Circle

Circles lack corners but Columbus Circle has many, including two, at Broadway and at Eighth Avenue, respectively, which have long been cursed. Between them stands 2 Columbus Circle. The building was commissioned by A & P heir Huntington Hartford, the kind of name which may very well breed curses, and was designed by Edward Durell Stone (MOMA, Kennedy Center) for a museum that would house his art collection, called the Gallery of Modern Art. The Gallery of Modern Art closed in 1969 and the building went unused between 1969-1980. By then, 2 Columbus Circle was owned by Gulf and Western, the California oil company, and was later gifted to the city for a hefty tax break. The Museum of Design continued the cursed tradition and has brought its bad juju into the present era. Even after the building's hand-wringing renovation in 2005, no New Yorker could be made to care about what goes on inside 2 Columbus Circle. Well, how could they? The curse would never allow for it.

The Northwest Corner of 57th Street and Sixth Avenue

The northwest corner of 57th and Sixth Avenue has been cursed for roughly twenty-five years. In the preceding period, it had been Wolf's Delicatessen. This wasn't the greatest pastrami sandwich in town, but Wolf's certainly knew what it was and showed some real character. Since Wolf's closure, there has been, among other things, a Delta 360 lounge. That's right, a Delta lounge, with all its powers of transporting you out of the Greatest City in the World back to the airport you landed in just days before upon arriving here. Brilliant. A brilliant failure, that is. But such is the power of the curse to dement the identity of a given corner. Bravo, curse. Bravo. You are powerful and have a wonderful sense of humor. An airport lounge, in Midtown. That's hilarious.

The Corners of Bleecker Street in Greenwich Village

MacDougal, Sullivan, and Thompson are streets that have long evoked romantic notions of a Freewheelin' Greenwich Village, and nowhere more so than at their Bleecker Street intersections. Unfortunately, the past twenty years have seen the area transformed into one of New York City's most cursed stretches, a pastiche of here-today gone-tomorrow grab-and-go food spots catering to NYU undergrads, souvenir-and-tchotchke tourist traps, and not much else. Yes, like Dylan in the eighties, this legendary folk corridor has completely lost its way. Whatever the fix, it won't be easy. But then exorcising the curse never is.

9

The Conversation

Being a family with a writer and a painter didn't leave much money for extra in our lives, and if we needed someone to watch Waylon, we could only afford the very cheapest babysitter in all of New York City:

Graham.

Celia convinced me of this, anyway, and didn't have a hard time doing so. It could have been the difference between us paying our bills on time or late or not at all. Graham said that he was only too happy to take care of Waylon. Spending time with Celia's son was important to him. He wanted to have a presence in the life of her child.

Celia and I had a friend's birthday dinner to attend one night, and when we returned home afterward, we found Graham on the phone arguing with his girlfriend, Nicole. Waylon was asleep in his crib. Celia and I checked on him, giving Graham some space. Still, we couldn't help but listen in on the call. Nicole didn't like Graham being here at Celia's apartment with Celia's son, didn't find it acceptable, considered it "abnormal." That was the word Graham uttered aloud, in disbelief.

"It's not abnormal. And no, I don't think of him as *my* child," said Graham. "Come on. That's foolish talk." I could see him struggling to compose his thoughts. "Stop saying that—I'm not playing father to him. No, no. I just told you. Well, maybe you never will understand."

In the bedroom, Celia turned to me and said, "Jeez. Maybe take Graham for a drink. Be a friend to him."

"Be a friend?"

"Yes, my love. You're good with relationships. You understand these things. Help him, please."

When Graham got off the phone, I asked him if he would like to go get a drink. He accepted, and for the first time ever we were on our own together, eventually walking into a bar on Metropolitan, a place of repurposed wood where the bartender, who was done up in the Victorian style—bowler hat, suspenders, waxed handlebar mustache—and his girlfriend were the only people present. We ordered whiskies and beers and took a booth in the back.

"She just doesn't get it," said Graham, "my bond with Celia isn't a threat to her."

"No, of course not. But maybe you can see where Nicole's coming from. Maybe building Waylon's nursery, which takes a whole lot of time and effort, and babysitting him at night instead of spending time with her, maybe it's creating some kind of...what's the word...*insecurity*, Graham. What do you think? Could there be anything to that?"

"I don't deny that there may be, Paul."

"Maybe Nicole doesn't always feel like the most important person in your life. Let me ask you a question: have you built *her* any dining tables or bookcases?"

Graham's look indicated no, and also that he didn't appreciate being asked. "To be honest, I don't think that would resolve anything for her, not as far as her feelings for Celia are concerned."

"You're probably right about that," I said. "But what I wonder is how Nicole must feel looking at you and Celia from the outside. Trying to understand what your relationship is all about must be very hard for her."

"Paul, my relationship with Celia is not hard to understand. It's about a deep connection. It's about a platonic love that cannot be broken."

"What if Nicole is afraid that you haven't actually moved on from your marriage with Celia? What if Nicole thinks you're still *in* love with Celia?"

"Then she would be wrong."

"Okay. But I have to imagine that you would have stayed married to Celia for the rest of your life if not for the fact that she decided that the marriage was over."

"Yes, I would have."

"Well, there you go."

"What's that supposed to mean?"

"To be on your end of that experience, that's a lot of pain, Graham. Most people would put some space between themselves and the source of that pain. They'd do it just to survive. That's not your way, though. You head right into the fire."

"Paul, there *is* no fire," he said.

"There isn't?"

"No."

At the middle of the table a candle burned in a small glass jar and Graham took the jar between thumb and forefinger, raising it to eye-level and smiling. This was an attempt at a joke. But then it was with the added light that I noticed Graham didn't look so well: pasty skin, dark bags under the eyes, a much-too-thin face. He had missed a patch of hair on his neck while shaving, almost unheard of for someone so fastidious about his appearance. Perhaps it was only an off day. He was saying to me, "That's what people just don't understand, Paul—there is no fire, no pain, just two very tightly bonded people who've been able to reimagine their relationship, to remake it in a fashion that better suits their needs at the present time. Celia and I, we love each other. We always will. There's nothing more to it. It's all very simple."

"So, you don't see any kind of struggle for you in this?"

"What struggle, Paul?"

"Maybe an imbalance of power?"

"What imbalance of power?"

"You're a very generous soul, Graham."

"Thank you, Paul. I appreciate that. Generosity is what guides me in my life. It always has been. I like to give. If there was something you needed that I could give to you right now, I would."

"No, no, please, Graham. No, you've given me enough. And I've got to hand it to you, you've got *something* figured out."

"I appreciate your saying so, Paul."

We got another round. The bar began to fill up—a man with his pit bull, a skateboarder, a rock 'n' roller, some art students. Graham put his fresh beer back in two long sips.

"Are you all right?" I said.

"I want to tell you something that's been on my mind for a long, long time, Paul. And I know it's going to be a sensitive subject, and you'll probably tell me that I've crossed the line in asking you."

"Now you're stressing *me* out."

Graham chuckled. He hadn't worn his Sherlock Holmes hat tonight, but he must have had it on earlier—there was a line of indentation straight across his forehead. With his thoughtful brown eyes narrowing, he said, "Paul, would you ever…would you…would you ever let me come along to find a cursed corner?"

Heat flashed through my chest. "I, well—"

Of all the things he might have asked me, I hadn't expected to get off so easily.

"I'm so sorry, Paul. I've overreached here. I apologize. It's just I've always wanted to ask you. But then I know it's a personal thing that you do and I don't mean to impose or—"

"No, no, not at all, Graham. I'd be honored to have you join me."

"That's so very kind of you. Because there's one just down the street from here that's been on my mind for as long as I've been reading your newsletter and I would just love to show it to you."

"You read the newsletter?"

"Of course, I do. I'm a big fan. I see cursed corners everywhere because of you, Paul. But this one corner—oh, this one—I'm dying to bring you there."

"Well, let's go have a look then. Come on."

"Right now?" said Graham.

"You said it's just down the street. I'd love to see it. Come, *let's go.*"

143 Roebling Street

Do you ever get that dead-inside feeling? Your heart, it's beating, but you feel a kind of emptiness there? You think to yourself that you had once been a more vibrant person with a life that felt vital, propulsive, but then you were left by the one you love and you had to snuff out all the feeling in your heart or else perish, and that act of suppression makes it so that now you're just floating along from day to day without any depth or meaning, without any feeling whatsoever? Well, say hello to 143 Roebling Street, who knows just how you feel. The five-story red brick warehouse was built in 1907 and up until not long ago had been occupied by dozens of artists, the building's Great Lovers. Between the 2000s and the 2010s, the Roebling Tea Room thrived on the ground floor, its industrial aesthetic and "local," "farm-to-table" menu pointing to the trends that lay ahead. The restaurant's red neon sign lighting up the corner was a beating heart keeping rhythm for the whole neighborhood. In 2014, however, the building was bought up by RedSky Capital for $32.3 million dollars, and that spelled the end for the Roebling Tea Room, as it did for the artists living in the apartments above whose leases, likewise, were not renewed.

"Goodbye, my lovers. It was good, was it not? And who will love me now? Someone? Anyone? No one?"

I am afraid not. The building, as well-located as any in one of the most desirable neighborhoods in all of New York City, has just gone into its sixth year of vacancy. Can everyone say cursed?

In 2019, looking for a new lover, the kind you go for when you've lost all self-worth and have forgotten what you used to be like in your better days, Los Angeles-based Calmwater Capital facilitated a $60 million refinancing of RedSky Capital's debt, an eighteen-month loan with a one-year option, to pay for further development costs to convert those lofts into offices and retail space. However, that wasn't the fix—in the years since, all units, including those commercial spaces on street-level, have remained vacant—and now the dread weighs heavier. The curse, indeed. It is written. What will lift it? Who knows? But hopefully something soon. The neighborhood is crying out for life in this one-time hub of Williamsburg. And 143 Roebling is feeling very lonely, wondering how long it must go on this way.

The next time you see her, be kind and say hello. Perhaps lean in and give a hug. She could use one.

10
Suspicion

I had to call my mother and check in. How long had it been since we last spoke? A month? Perhaps longer. Gathering the mail in the poorly lit vestibule and climbing the stairs, I dialed her. She never answered the first time I called, could never stop whatever it was she was doing and get to the phone in time. Sometimes her cell was in another room or at the bottom of her purse and I would have to call back again straight away if I hoped to get her on the line. That remained true now.

"Paul, are you okay? Is something wrong? I'm very busy and I have to call you back. Unless you need something. Is there an emergency?"

"No, I just realized we haven't spoken for a while, and I wanted to say hi and make sure that you were doing okay."

"Paul, this really isn't a good time. I have a new mattress coming into my room. Can I call you back? Will you be around later?"

"Yes."

"I'll call you tonight. Oh wait, not tonight. Tonight I have dinner plans with Marco, the bellhop. How about in the morning?"

"The morning works. Or we could just meet in person? I could come to the Carlyle and we could do breakfast. I could bring the baby."

"No, no, that won't work. We'll find time. Also, I saw Celia walking down the street with a young woman yesterday, a redhead."

"Really? In your neighborhood?"

"Yes."

"Hmm. Strange. But you didn't say hello?"

"*No*, because she was on the other side of the avenue and she was walking with a stranger and I didn't have the time or energy to meet someone new."

"Understood, Mom."

"Kisses to my grandchild. Bye now."

I came in the front door and tossed the mail on the stand. There was Celia at the dining table, filing her nails. The sound—*shh-shh, shh-shh, shh-shh*—immediately put me on edge.

"My mother said she saw you walking yesterday on the Upper East Side. She said that you were with someone."

"Really? She saw me?" said Celia, eyes focused on her nails, the file moving swiftly back and forth.

"I didn't realize you weren't alone, that you were out with someone."

Celia was working hard on a particular nail, eyes half-shut, bottom lip curled so tightly to have almost disappeared.

"Are you going to tell me who it was?" I said.

"Sure," said Celia, taking up a pink buffer now. "Her name is Anne Noel."

"Ah, Anne Noel. And who's that?"

"Anne is a cultural critic."

"A cultural critic? Is that what you just said?"

"She's also a new friend."

"A cultural critic and a new friend. Great."

Beneath serious dark eyes, Celia smiled. "Anne's husband is an investor at the Regency Gallery."

"Okay," I said, "now I see." Or I thought I did, anyway.

She told me there was an opening tonight and that we should have Graham babysit and both go. A part of me wanted to point out to Celia that it was odd to say that you had been somewhere and done something and to have failed to mention that you had been not alone but with someone. Generally speaking, the difference between being by oneself or being accompanied by someone else was significant. What distracted me from the subject was Celia's interest in the Regency Gallery. More than any other gallery in New York, Celia wanted to show there. That Anne's husband helped finance the operation filled me with some hope. Perhaps this Anne Noel could be of use. Celia shrugged at the suggestion, not because she didn't agree. It was merely the old subject of gallery representation and the aggravation of it. I didn't press her, but I was not ready to give up on my optimism, either. What if Anne Noel's husband did pull a string and give her a show? What if? And who was to say it wouldn't happen with some ease? Who you knew and what they were willing to do for you was the very basis of making any progress in the art world (and in *any* world, for that matter). So then why not Anne and her husband?

Later, in the large, packed gallery space, standing with Anne and her husband, Leon, and his business partner, Niles, who co-owned and managed the Regency, I immediately lost all hope of Celia's finding a way in with these people. We were standing together under a larger-than-life doormat sewn by the artist whose show had gone up this evening. The shag piece appeared to have been vomited-on. Anne and Leon were asking Niles about the inspiration for the work and how long it had taken the artist to make. Once all the small talk had died down and the five of us were grasping for the next subject to discuss, I began to wait impatiently for Anne, a freckled redhead in a black leather miniskirt and iridescent tube top with the Wall Street husband on her arm, to say something about Celia's work to the gallerist, Niles—something about how talented Celia was and how Niles should have a studio visit and see her paintings, or how Anne and Leon were already considering the purchase of a painting in a new series by Celia, or how Celia was a million times better than the artist whose work hung on these very walls. Yes, something about how if you really compared the vomited-on doormat to Celia's work, you would see right away that this artist had almost no talent whatsoever.

Something to that effect.

But Anne was leaving Celia out in the cold with the gallerist. Maybe I was being too impatient. Yes, Anne would get around to all of that in time. But to think, Anne hadn't even introduced Celia to Niles *as* an artist in the first place. And this was a friend?

"Niles, are you familiar with Celia's paintings?" I interrupted. "She does mostly figurative work of women."

"Oh, yeah?" said Niles, tall, slim, blond. "You paint with oils?" he said, to Celia.

"I do," she replied.

And that was all Celia had needed: a way in.

Leon, black slicked back hair, full dark beard, bearish chest, seemed pleased that Celia and Niles were talking now. Meanwhile, Anne's gaze began moving about the gallery, avoiding me. Then she said, "Will you excuse me? I see someone I have to say hello to."

Leon stood aside so that Anne could pass. The husband— he had a sleepy kind of bloodhound warmth about him. I knew deep down that he didn't want to be here either, even if it was his money keeping the doors open.

"Celia and Anne have been spending a lot of time together these days," said Leon.

"Have they?"

"They *have*," said Leon. He was still in his work suit. A sweaty, stout figure, he seemed like he could use some air.

"That's interesting. So they've become good friends?"

"Yes. I'm sorry, did you not know?" said Leon.

"I just found out about Anne today. I guess Celia's been keeping her from me."

"Don't blame Celia. It's Anne. She does this with people."

"Does what?"

"She doesn't like to share her friends. She prefers people one-on-one. That's her thing. Always has been."

"Well, that's good to know."

"She just needs a lot of personal attention."

The following day, Celia began a portrait of Anne. Though this wasn't her first attempt at a new painting since Waylon's birth, to see Celia back at work was absolutely thrilling. In the studio, before a canvas with a paint brush in her hand—*that* was where she belonged. The canvas was average size, about twenty by twelve inches. Anne was situated at the middle with a horse beside her and two men peering down from a window above. I didn't like the painting. It was this Anne. Her presence, it irritated me. But Celia finished the painting in a week and after it dried, she gave it to Anne and her husband as a gift. This was much too generous, and I told her so while the two of us were lying in bed one night. Anne and Leon were wealthy, they should have to buy the painting.

"They'll hang it on their wall, and you never know who will see it," said Celia. "I'm sure Niles, the gallerist, goes by their place from time to time. And then once Anne has something of mine to show people, once she owns something, she'll be much more likely to talk me up to people, important people—gallerists and so on. Anne just has to feel like she's involved, like she's got a piece of it, you know?"

"Sure. I do."

"You have to find a way to let people in. But then you also have to let *them* think that they've entered on their own volition. It's very tricky, though, isn't it, Paul? But everyone likes to receive a beautiful painting. That's easy. What? Oh, please, don't look at me like that. This is business. I have to get my career going. I have a family to feed."

Park and 75

Curse, are you in the pocket of the artworld? Tell the truth. Today, I went uptown to Park and 75—and now I just have to ask.

Owned by Gagosian, Park and 75 is certainly the most ambitious enterprise to ever occupy the location. Previously a children's boutique, this corner has always been a kind of ghost town unto itself as dreamt up by Edward Hopper. Charming yet unnoticeably quiet, one business after another, after another, has failed here. I know it's you, Curse, lurking in the walls. But presumably, Gagosian is the perfect next tenant up, for the blue-chip gallery doesn't need to make even one sale to survive but can afford to play it cool and live under the radar and use the space as just more advertising for its brand. Yes, the gallery has the means to stay put as long as it likes—forever, presumably—unless, that is, you force Gagosian to exit, dear Curse? Which is why I ask if you are in the pocket of the artworld. Well, are you? You, too, can be bought, is that it? Everyone has a price, so, what's yours?

11
Trust

A friend was celebrating the publication of a new novel and the party was being held at the West Village home of a wealthy patron in the kind of townhouse a person might dream of living in one day and could go on dreaming of because it was not likely to happen. The backyard rivaled the Conservatory Gardens in Central Park. Word had it that some of the musicians performing swing on the parlor floor were the only ones Quincy Jones would hire on a recording session. The bar was as many feet long as my apartment and there was no shortage of champagne, scotch, and ice-cold vodka. The caviar had its own station and tuxedoed attendant. I had come alone tonight, Celia having stayed home with Waylon. The guest of honor, Leah Crane, a petite blonde in a long red dress, was the author of three novels and two short story collections, a star straight out of Bennington College.

Saying hello now, Leah held me in her arms, not letting go. "I miss you," she said. "How are you?"

"Glad to be here."

It had been two months since we'd last seen one another. It was a run-in on the street in SoHo. Celia and Waylon were with me. I made it quick. Walking away afterward, Celia said that that woman, whoever she was, wanted to sleep with me. I denied it, but Celia assured me that I was wrong and that she knew when a woman wanted to sleep with a man.

"Congratulations on the book, Leah."

"Thank you. *Come*. I want you to meet some people."

Leah took my hand and led me off into the crowd. She introduced me to one person after another, never once letting go and always referring to us as very good old friends though we hadn't known one another that long. All the while, Leah's hand seemed to stake claim to something more. People might have thought we were together the way Leah let her arm sit around my waist or rested her head on my shoulder.

"Paul writes a great newsletter on cursed corners," said Leah. She was speaking to several guests in the garden.

"A newsletter? How cute," said one woman.

"I don't know it," said a man beside her.

"Sounds scary," said another.

"You're not wrong," said Leah. "It is a little frightening."

"I like your newsletter." It was the host of the party, Rick Miller, dark crew cut, red bowtie, black suit, a face shaped like an onion.

"You've heard of it? I'm shocked," I said.

"I'm *in* real estate, and yes," said Miller, "I know your newsletter. I also know that you've made a lot of enemies around town. You're not very good for property value."

Everyone laughed. Did they know why they were laughing?

Leah whispered in my ear that I better not try and leave early, that she wouldn't let me. I told her I wouldn't and then stared down into my whiskey glass and shot it back. What time was it, anyway?

At the next moment, Miller began speaking to me about some of the properties that had appeared in my newsletter and of how the owners had indeed complained to him about me. "You really should be careful. Honestly, Paul, these properties you're writing about are owned by some pretty dangerous people."

"Good journalism always assumes a bit of risk."

"Sure, sure," said Miller, clasping his hands behind his back. "But you're not a journalist. What you write is an industry newsletter."

"True."

"You don't want to die because of something so insignificant, do you?"

"*Die?*" I said, going cold. "Who said anything about dying?"

"Listen, just take my advice and tread a little more lightly here. Otherwise, who knows, you may find yourself in a bad situation."

The musicians could be heard through the open parlor window playing Count Basie.

Miller, gritting his teeth—they were brittle, brown teeth that looked like they could break apart in his mouth—took me by the wrist and said, "Are you okay, Paul? Do you need help?"

"Ah, yes…ah, you could tell me where the bathroom is?"

"Sure thing." Miller pointed directly past my shoulder. "It's just through those doors and to the left."

"Thank you."

I stepped back—and Leah tugged on me.

"Where are you going?" she said. Her hand moved to my cheek now. She stared into my eyes.

"To the bathroom."

"Hurry back to me," she said and then kissed me on the mouth.

The kiss startled me. "I will."

Two minutes later I was in a taxi, heading home. Because of construction on the Williamsburg Bridge, the ride took twice as long as usual, almost forty minutes. When I came in the door, Celia was reading in bed. I was so grateful to find her awake. I washed up and got into bed and was at the next moment cleaving to her body.

"Hi, baby," she said, stroking my head, eyes still in her book. "How was your night?"

"I love you."

"I love you, too."

I lifted my head. "I want you to know that I don't need anything from the world out there. I have it all right here, in this home."

"That's right, you do," she said.

For a while we lay just like that, with Celia holding a book in one hand and running her fingers through my hair with the other, and to me this bed felt like the safest place in the world.

By afternoon the following day, however, after family-time—breakfast and the playground, then the grocery store followed by lunch—Celia went to look at art with Anne, and with Waylon playing in his bedroom, I immediately got on the phone with Leah and explained my disappearance of the night before.

Leah said that she had already decided never to see me again but that she was listening, yes—and what did I have to say for having ruined her night? I was surprised by Leah's anger, and I didn't have much to say for myself, as it were. The senselessness of this conversation distracted me. After coming in the door last night so relieved to find Celia—my love, the mother of my child, my very best friend—so happy to see her and to have *this* life, I had allowed for the two of us to slide away from each other again. I could have told Celia not to go to the museum with Anne because *I* had to be with her today. I could have said that. Likewise, I could have hung up on Leah right now and cut her off for good.

Instead, I began to apologize.

"How will you make it up to me?" asked Leah.

"What's that?"

"You can't just apologize and expect me to forgive you. So, how will you make it up to me?"

Waylon called out from the other end of the apartment. I said, "I'll give it some thought. I definitely *will* make it up to you. My child is about to jump from the top of a bookcase. Let me help him avert catastrophe and we'll pick up this conversation soon."

"We better, Paul."

"I'm really sorry about last night, Leah," I said, instantly regretting it.

"Good. Because I'm going to be your post-divorce rebound second wife."

"*What?*"

"I'm joking. Jesus. Go save your kid."

Waylon wasn't on a bookcase but with his feet on the floor, pants pulled up past his belly button, clapping his hands and chanting, "Dad, Dad, Dad, Dad, Dad."

"Yes, yes," I said, "I'm here. I'm right here with you."

We sat down together and began stacking blocks, one on top of the other, to my son's delight. But no more than a minute later, a restless sort of energy took hold of me. I could feel it all surging in my chest. I couldn't remain here playing with blocks. I had to get out of the apartment, to be in motion, to do something to displace this agitation.

"Come on, kid, we're going out. Come on, come on, let's go find some of our favorite corners, the ones that aren't cursed. We love that game, don't we? That'll fix our mood. Don't cry. We'll play more with our blocks as soon as we get back."

The Favorite Corners

I was dragging my son around the city today, looking at some of our favorite corners—those very successful corners that are in no way under the influence of the curse—and it occurred to me that it would be nice to share some of them with you. After all, this column could use a little balance in its life.

Our first stop was at one of the finest corners of them all at 73rd and Third Avenue, the original JG Melons. What a heartbreaker!

I desperately wanted one of their famous cheeseburgers and a beer or two, but the line was out the door and I didn't have the patience for a long wait. I tried to play the child-card with the host, but that got me nowhere. My son said something to me to the effect of, "Dad, can we please go home?" But I said, "Not yet, my child. We've just gotten started and there are more of our favorite corners to see."

I strolled him about a mile to the corner of Madison Avenue and 57th Street to I.M Pei's IBM Building. A total knockout—we marveled at its cantilevered entryway for a long while until one of us fell asleep.

With the child out cold, this was my chance to shuttle him anywhere I liked. And being that it was just one of those days where I felt I had to keep on moving for hours and hours on end, the child's sleep-state felt like a great gift. All of a sudden, or so it seemed, we were many miles from the wonder of the IBM Building at the corner of Spring and West at a salt shed for the Department of Sanitation designed by Dattner Architects and WXY Architecture and Urban Design. But how had I gotten here? I could hardly remember all the streets in between. But boy, I woke up in a kind of fantasy, reveling at the vision of an absolute beauty, a truly inspired architectural performance, a building that shows what a corner can be and lifts up my soul.

After the salt shed, I finally gave into my child and took him home just as the sun was starting to set. But then as I sat him down before his blocks, I made an appeal to the Curse, said it under my breath:

"Dear Curse, as it pertains to our favorite corners, don't even try it. Just stay back. Leave them alone, goddamnit. You've got so many corners as it is, do you really need more? Are you so greedy? Spare us these corners, for they are too loveable. Don't ruin them for us. And don't complicate our feelings by telling us that you'll come around eventually one day, that you always do, because nothing is forever. We must think in terms of permanence. So just spare us these few corners. What do you say? Can we agree that you won't meddle there? Can we? If your answer is no, then give me a sign, any sign, okay? I'll know it's you, Curse."

12

In Truth

"Do you ever fool around with other women, Paul?"

"Do I ever fool around with other women?"

"*Yes*. Do you?"

"Do I fool around with other women?"

"Yes. Do you fool around with other women?"

"I don't understand the question."

"What don't you understand about it?"

"Quite possibly every single aspect of the question. It's all beyond my understanding."

"Well, maybe you're over thinking it? Let me try it again: do you fool around with other women?"

"I still don't understand. I have no idea what you're talking about."

Celia and I were at a sushi bar early on a summer's evening. Though the small pocket restaurant would be bustling in an hour, we were the first and only customers. All the same, feeling a lack of privacy, I looked over one shoulder and then the other and whispered my denial.

"Have you grown suspicious of me? Has someone told you something?"

"No," said Celia, playing with the strap of her blue overalls, eyes focused on a point in front of her, a piece of octopus or tuna behind the glass. She smiled. "I just wonder sometimes. I know women must come onto you."

"No. They don't."

"Oh, come on," she said, pointing at her sake glass. To refill her own was considered bad luck. I took the carafe, topped her off. "And really, I'm not accusing you of anything. I'm just asking because sometimes I wonder, that's all."

"You wonder about me?"

"Yes. But also I think about life being long and monogamy and whether it is possible for two people to be just with each other forever. I don't know if it is. I'm sure the day will come when you *will* fool around with another woman."

"Oh, you're so sure of it, are you?"

"Yes."

"I am a monogamist. That's a fact."

"Are you, though?"

The waitress, a young Japanese woman, was standing behind us, ready to take our order.

"We're going to need a minute," I said.

Celia held up the menu. "Sorry, we haven't even looked."

The waitress went to stand at the front door.

"Whatever I am, I haven't been with any other women, and I have no plans to be with any other women."

"Yes, but we're young, and again, you just don't know. You don't know what will happen."

"Fine, I'll give you that. But I feel certain."

"Of course—and being with the same person forever is a lovely idea. But if you couldn't do it, if you weren't able to do it for some reason, because something happened, because someone threw herself on you and you took the opportunity and went for it—I just want you to know that you don't have to tell me about it. It's okay. I don't want to hear anything about any of it."

"So, no written reports?"

Celia pinched me. She was being serious.

"Celia, are you trying to tell me right now that you've already been with someone?"

"What? *No*," said Celia, her hand coming to rest on my shoulder. "No, no, no, no, no. I haven't been with anyone else. I'm just talking about a *what-if*."

"Okay, fine. *Good*. Let's entertain thoughts of all kinds of unpleasant scenarios, shall we?"

"Paul, I'm just talking about the kinds of things that happen when you're alive and living in the world. Things happen. I just think we can be higher minded now and discuss the subject like two mature adults."

I drank the sake all the way down and then tapped my glass. Celia filled me back up. I said, "I'm not getting together with any other women."

"But maybe you *would* if you encountered the right woman."

"You are my right woman. There is no other."

"Well, that's very sweet," she said.

"I mean it. No one can just replace you and the feelings I have for you."

"Do you promise?"

"Yes, I promise. And I love our family. I would never do anything to jeopardize what we have. Never. Ever."

But then Celia said she didn't know if she could say the same about herself. She distrusted herself, carried a horrible fear that someday down the line she would do something with someone that would bring severe, irreversible damage to everything we had. "I'm honestly afraid of whether I can be faithful and remain committed to a relationship forever. I worry that one day I'll fall in love with someone else. I know it's terrible to hear. I'm not trying to hurt you. I'm just being honest."

"Stop, please."

"Paul, you have to know this. I'm committed to us, to our family. But we're still just in our early thirties. We have the rest of our lives yet to come. Do you really think that neither one of us will ever cross paths with a person who'll turn us on our heads?"

"*Stop.*"

"Okay, okay," she said, touching her hand to my face. "I love you. I love our life together. This is the only life I want. I don't mean to make you worry, and I don't want to upset you. We're *just* talking."

"Well, what do you want from me? What do you want to hear?"

"Just tell me you love me."

"I love you," I said. "Now, please, this conversation is making me ill. Can we talk about something else?"

13

A Trip to Paris

In the dark bedroom, Celia rolled off me and then hopped along down the hall with a kind of lightness of foot. She went to the bathroom, came back, and lay with one arm across my chest. Ever since our conversation on monogamy, we had been having a lot of sex. And yet every time something about it felt wrong, or else crucial, as if we needed the sex as a kind of panacea for something that we had not yet named or even spoken about. I couldn't say why I felt this way. It was here, though, this pressure on our sex. That I could say for sure.

And now Celia was telling me about a trip to Paris she would like to take with Anne.

"There's a big opening at the Pompidou. She has a room at the Ritz. She says I can stay there with her."

"Sounds nice. When is it?"

"That's the thing, it's actually very soon. I'd be leaving the day after tomorrow. And it's okay if you don't want me to go."

"I mean, I don't want to stop you from going. I guess it really doesn't matter how soon it is."

"That's kind of what I was thinking. What's the difference whether it's this week or next month? And you wouldn't mind taking care of Waylon for four days? Graham could help you."

"No, no, that's not necessary."

"Then is it settled?"

A trip to Paris with Anne Noel. Good for Celia. Why not. I had never been to Paris with Celia, but that Anne Noel could have that opportunity shouldn't be made into a big deal. I wouldn't be so sentimental. We had traveled to plenty of other great cities. Mostly within the United States, but over oceans, too. Just never to Paris, never there, no. Naturally, as two people in love, we talked about how wonderful it would be to one day go to Paris together and have the romantic experience that that city promised, but that Anne had slipped ahead of me in the Paris-line was not something to harp on. It was something to drop, to move on from, to disregard altogether, being that I was not a child and had to take life as it came and accept that travel-fantasies often played out not quite as happily as one would have hoped they would.

Celia flew off to Paris. Later the same day—with the time 3:15 p.m. in New York, 9:15 p.m. in the City of Light—and I had yet to hear from her. No call, no text, not even a *ping* to let me know that she had arrived safely. I spent the morning with Waylon, going up and down the Bowery in search of cursed corners. Distracted by the job, the kid, the traffic on Houston, I could almost forget about Celia and the fact that she had yet to be in touch. By the time I arrived home and put the child down for a nap, I *had* to know if she were alive or if something awful had happened to her.

I texted her: "R U O K?"

Four letters and a single question mark, concise, not overly prying, a message that acknowledged in its brevity that she was off in another country having an adventure and taking some space for herself from her family and her life in New York while still making it clear that I was concerned for her well-being.

Two more quiet hours passed.

Perhaps she'd just lost her phone. She was alive, but her phone had been left behind in a taxi. On the other hand, there was Anne's phone and if Celia could borrow it for just one moment to check in with me—as that was what a person did with their families after traveling on a plane to another country, a person called to say that all was fine and well—*this* would have been appreciated. But Celia didn't call that night, didn't text or email. And when by the following day I still hadn't heard from her, I dialed up the Ritz but could get no information on whether Celia and Anne had even checked in. I was ready to start trying random hospitals in Paris.

Before I could dial one, Leah called.

"What are you doing?" she asked me.

When I told her, she began to laugh. "Get ahold of yourself," she said. "Celia's off in Paris with her friend and she doesn't want to think about you and the kid. Do her a favor, let her forget her life for a second. Give her space."

"I'm trying. But not even a text? You've got to let a person know you're alive."

"She's alive. You're alive. *We're* alive. And you still owe me from the night of my book party."

Graham reported for babysitting duty at 7:00 p.m., and I got to Leah's in Chelsea at just after eight. Ringing her buzzer, waiting in the hallway for her to let me in, I thought of having sex with Leah in her kitchen the instant she opened the door, with clothes not removed but Leah's skirt lifted and my pants lowered and our shoes still on but underwear slid down and Leah on the kitchen counter beside a toaster and me leaning over her at the silverware drawer—I saw it all so clearly.

"Hold on a second," said Leah, from inside the apartment. "I'm coming, I'm coming." At last the door opened, and Leah stepped out into the hallway and closed the door behind her. We weren't going inside, she said. Her apartment was a mess. "Come, let's go."

Back on the night of her book party, Leah had just gotten a blow dry and was wearing a brand-new red dress. Now her blonde hair was wet and slicked back and her candy-cane striped dress was the only clean thing she claimed to have in her closet. She had made a reservation at a West Village tapas bar so small that it could only sit ten people right on top of one another and the mariachi player was right in your face, and the bartender in a tight white shirt with long black hair and goatee screamed for your drink order without even looking you in the eye while *he* made the tapas. I couldn't hear Leah, but perhaps that was a good thing.

"You think she's having an affair, right?" Leah shouted.

"I didn't say that."

"But she hasn't called you for three days?"

"Yes."

"Well, then *that's* an affair."

"You said over the phone that she was just taking space for herself."

"Yes, and that's the kind of space she's taking: affair-space." Leah clapped for the mariachi player, who was tuning up his instrument. She then handed him a twenty-dollar bill. "For you, for you," she said. "Bravo. You are a beautiful artist, stunning, just stunning. Paul, I'm not trying to upset you. But from what I understand of Celia, from what *you've* told me, she seems like a pretty free-spirited woman. Wasn't she in an open marriage when you met her?"

"She was, but—"

"And does she believe in monogamy?"

"Believe in it? No, I guess she doesn't."

Clutching a straw in her mouth, Leah drank a glass of sangria right down to the bottom. She said, "If she was in one open marriage, that tells me she doesn't believe in the conventional kind of one-person-for-every-one-person sort of thing, but maybe goes by a whole other method. I don't know her. I can't say. I'm just thinking about the kinds of things you've told me about her. I'm going off of that, okay? Bartender. Tequila, please! And that's okay, right? She loves you. You have a beautiful son together. You enjoy each other. What more do you want? You want *all* of her? You need to possess her?"

"No. I don't need to possess her, but—"

Four tequila shots landed on the table in front of me.

"Two for you, two for me," she said. Shooting back the first, Leah became momentarily convex and then wiped her mouth with her forearm and let out a gasp. "Wow, that's good. But let me ask you, who'd Celia go away with? A friend, right?"

"Maybe you've met her before. She's a cultural critic. Her name is Anne Noel."

"Anne Noel? Oh, God, not her. Anyone but her."

"You know Anne?"

"Yes, from *around*. But she once tried to steal a boyfriend away from me. Thing is, she doesn't even like men. It was just about winning against me. Who cares, right? But oh wow, that Anne Noel, she is a demented, sociopathic, hostile vampire fuck-suck piece of shit and you should know that she may be married to the hedge fund guy, but she likes women."

"Well, good. Celia likes men, so—"

"Anne is a very persuasive person."

"Leah, can't we talk about anything else?"

"Like what? You've got a real problem on your hands. I'm trying to help you. What else could you possibly want to talk about, Paul?"

"Anything," I said. The mariachi player was holding his guitar almost at my ear.

"Well," said Leah, wrapping her arms up around the back of her head, "what about us? I was sure we would have had sex by now."

"Leah, you're my friend."

"Just your friend? That's so boring. Celia's off having an affair in Paris. You could at least make out with me in a bar tonight. It's why I'm getting us all these drinks. I'm trying to get you drunk, Paul, so that we can finally do it."

"Leah. Wait. Hold on," I said. I was digging my phone out of my pocket. "*Celia*, she just texted me." I opened the message: a selfie of Celia and Anne in front of the Eiffel Tower. "Doing well, having a ball!" she had written. I made some attempt to conceal the image from Leah, but she had already seen it.

"Is that what I think it is? Show me. Show that to me right now." I handed Leah the phone and watched her face change. "Oh Paul, I'm sorry. You really are in trouble now. We should have a night to rival theirs, what do you say? Have you been to the Plaza since they renovated?"

"I think I have to go home."

"Home? Don't go home," said Leah, grabbing my hand. "Let's go to the Plaza. Even just to have a look. I haven't been for years. Come on, don't be such a bore!"

The Plaza Hotel

The Plaza Hotel is cursed. Truman Capote's spirit, drunk on three martinis, wouldn't even consider stepping through its doors, let alone hosting a Black and White Ball there. But for decade upon decade, you could feel the strongest of pulses beating at the corner of 59th Street off Fifth Avenue. There was Life. The High Life! The revolving doors at the entrance were in constant motion. The Oak Room smelled of gin and money. The grand marble lobby was loud with the chatter of humans giddy from pheromones and adrenaline, cocaine and champagne, glitz. Then the storied hotel went semi-residential in 2005, and almost immediately the most important of all New York City's hotels lost its voice. Had it gone hoarse? Did it have strep? It certainly needed a doctor. Or perhaps an exorcist? The curse was no doubt present and has been ever since, dictating from its perch on the hotel's mansard roof. (Where else would it sit?) When I look at the building now, I see nothing but a handsome coffin. What can be done? The forces—private equity groups, the money laundering of international criminals—are too strong. Will we ever see the Plaza Hotel restored to its former glory? Will the curse ever allow for it? Just to ask makes me tremble.

PART 3

14

Run for Your Life

A successful Polish painter, Nadia Kowalski, had been after Celia for at least a year to come to Poland and work for her by painting some of the finer details of her paintings. Nadia's studio was in the countryside, a little more than an hour outside Krakow, in Rabka. She had offered to fly Waylon and I out so that we could be there with Celia. Nadia had a beautiful, sprawling farmhouse with plenty of spare rooms and when the job was finished, we were welcome to travel south to her seaside apartment on the northern coast of Croatia, where we could stay for as long as we liked, *gratis*.

Poland didn't quite have the ring of a France or Spain, but as Celia pointed out, we would be in Europe and could easily travel throughout the continent. Looking at a map, we charted a route from Krakow south to Croatia. We would hit Slovakia, Austria, Slovenia. From Pula, Croatia, where Nadia's seaside apartment was located on a narrow medieval street facing the Adriatic, we were but a short drive to Trieste and could slip down to Venice and Florence, Rome—all of Italy. Celia had declined the job offer twice before. She and I had both been busy with other things. It hadn't felt like the right time. Now

I urged Celia to get back in touch with Nadia, to take the offer and bring the whole family overseas. Celia and I needed this trip; we were on a dangerous path and going off to Europe would mean escaping something awful. Since returning from Paris three months ago, Celia had been pulling away more and more. Toward Anne? They *were* together a lot, going to an event or out to tea or to a museum. Celia had painted many more portraits of her, too. And was their relationship romantic? I was not yet convinced. As far as I knew, Celia had never been with a woman. Regardless, Celia and I required time away together—dedicated time—and Poland would allow us to take that moment and regain some control over our lives.

Celia emailed Nadia to discuss the plan. Right away, Nadia, who had a big art show coming up and was desperate for help, said she was on board. August 1st, Celia, Waylon, and I would fly to Krakow. Nadia would put us up in a hotel for a night and then her studio assistant, Dominika, would drive us out to Rabka, where we would remain until the 16th—two weeks in the countryside outside Krakow—after which Nadia would lend us her spare car and we would head down to Croatia and stay as long as we liked in her apartment in Pula, travel as far and wide as we desired from there, and then return to Rabka, drop the car, and fly out of Krakow back to the US. Celia and I were thrilled. Europe for a month, and with most expenses covered and even money earned.

On the night before our flight, falling asleep in bed, Celia surprised me by saying how much she and I—our relationship—would benefit from this time away together.

She had been feeling it, too.

—

The flight from New York to Krakow took about eight hours. It was 9:00 a.m. when we arrived. A chauffeur in a black suit stood in the atrium just beyond customs with a sign that read "Celia and Family." His name was Aleksandr, and he insisted on carrying our luggage to the car. Nadia was putting us up in a Holiday Inn in the Old Town, just minutes from the main square, Rynek Glowny. If the hotel made up the full extent of our travels, Waylon would have been greatly satisfied all the same—the automatic sliding doors admitted the small child into a lobby with seemingly all the pleasures in the world, with a plate of tart candies on the concierge desk and a television above the lobby bar airing Scooby Doo (in Polish). In fact, all three of us were content. The room was well-arrayed, with a comfortable queen bed and an additional twin-sized roll-in for Waylon. It was clean with a full bath, good light, a fully stocked mini bar, cable television, and much to explore just beyond the doors. But first, a nap. Celia drew the curtains, the room went dark, and the three of us fell asleep together in the bed.

Sometime later, the hotel phone started ringing. Celia was nearest and she answered. The bedside clock read 5:30 p.m. I listened closely to Celia, who gave the details of our flight, the drive in from the airport, and our satisfaction with the hotel accommodations. I assumed it was Nadia on the line, but it turned out to be her studio assistant, Dominika, who had come in from the farmhouse in Rabka to drive us back out there tomorrow. She asked if we were available for dinner tonight, and Celia and I were happy to accept her invitation.

I threw open the curtains, light pouring into the hotel room, and then went to shower. We were meeting in two hours at a restaurant Dominika promised was one of the best in Krakow. Under the spray of hot water and soaping myself up, I reckoned that I was getting away with something extraordinary. Here we were, the whole family in Europe together for the first time, at the start of a wonderful adventure. Far from our busy New York lives, Celia and I would give one another proper attention. This was a gift, one that would fill us up for years and years to come.

Some twenty minutes later, out in the big square, with its cobble stones, Gothic archways, and magnificent cathedral, its fountains and monuments and museums, as exquisite and sprawling as any in Eastern Europe, and with the sun still out and the early-evening warm, Waylon chased after large bubbles sent floating through the air by a man with a tremendous wooden wand that he dipped in a bucket of soapy water. With an hour until we were to meet Dominika, we sat in a café with two glasses of red wine and a hot chocolate for Waylon, each of us lifted by the splendor of our surroundings and the sense of possibility they promised.

Celia reached across the table and took my hand. "Can you believe all this?" she said. "We've made it. I love you."

"I love you," I said.

The restaurant was on the other side of the Vistula from the Old Town, and we rode in a taxi through the city, staring out the window and taking in the sights, Waylon on his mother's lap, a long-haired child with the summer wind on his face.

"Welcome to Krakow," said Dominika, upon arriving at the restaurant just minutes after us. She collapsed into the one unoccupied seat, accidentally dumping the contents of her leather bag under the dining table—lipstick, lighter, keys, coins—then getting down on her knees to collect it all. Celia and I exchanged a look, laughing quietly with one another. Dominika was tall, blonde, blue-eyed, with a long straight nose. She wore a tank top, blue jeans, and black cowboy boots. Her voice was deep and raspy.

She said, "Nadia likes to call me by my full name, Dominika, but I prefer to go by Dom."

"*Dom*," said Waylon, enjoying the single syllable.

She winked at the child. "That's right, kiddo."

"Where you from, Dom?" asked Celia. "I don't hear a Polish accent."

"No. I'm from Detroit," she said, wrapping her thumbs inside the waist of her blue jeans. "My parents are still in Michigan, but my parents' parents are all from here."

"From Poland?" I said.

"From right here in Krakow."

"And how long have you worked for Nadia?" asked Celia.

"*Too* long." Again she winked, this time at me, before smiling at Celia. But Dom said it was a good gig, especially for a young upstart artist like herself. Nadia was very supportive of Dom's photography career and helped her land shows and introduced her to collectors, not just in Poland but throughout Europe and the world. "Nadia Kowalski, she picks up a phone and people listen. Her work flies out of the studio. She's a star."

"She sure is," said Celia.

The menu was much like what we would find back in Williamsburg, farm-to-table fare with no traces of a Polish influence. When Celia and I pointed this out, Dom told us not to worry, we would have plenty of opportunity to eat garlic soup and mashed potatoes and chicken cutlets out in Rabka. Now was the time to relish some variety.

After dinner, Dom said she would be happy to show us around for a few hours, to have a stroll down by the Vistula.

"It's a lovely offer," I said. "But I'm so tired. I've hit a wall. You and Celia can keep going, if you like, and I'll take Waylon back with me."

We were at the head of a bridge crossing and a stone stairway leading down to the banks of the river. The sun had almost set. A tugboat moved slowly along the calm, uncrowded waterway.

"Well, Celia, shall we?"

"No, no," she said. "If Paul and Waylon are going back, I'm going with them."

"Suit yourself," said Dom. "Tomorrow, as they say, is another day. As for me, it looks like I'll be going it alone. I bid you all a goodnight."

15

Countryside Idyll

The next morning at eleven, Dom pulled up outside the hotel in Nadia's white Mercedes sedan ready to drive us out to the house in Rabka. She invited Celia to sit up front in the passenger seat next to her, but Celia declined—she would take the back with Waylon and let me sit up front. Dom, twisting her face at Celia, said, "All right, suit yourself, babe."

The GPS estimated about a two-hour trip, but Dom was aggressive behind the wheel, and we were making excellent time. Along the highway, the scenery beyond the city limits was not unlike that which you'd see outside New York with urban landscape shifting to suburban, but the smaller roads drew the beautiful rolling hills and farmland as green and lush as you'd find anywhere into relief. It was half past twelve when we pulled up at the blue wooden gate at the foot of Nadia's driveway. Dom said, "We're here. I'll bring your bags up to your rooms. You just head in. Follow the stone path up to the backdoor of the house. You'll see it."

The large house reminded me at once of Melikhovo, Anton Chekhov's estate where *The Seagull* and *Uncle Vanya* were written—a two-story structure painted an almost identical shade of pink and with the same oxidized green metal roof. Before we could get to the top of the stone stairs, Celia took my hand, pulling me close to her.

"This place is stunning," she said. "We'll be so happy here."

"We will," I said.

Two windows overhead burst open then and Dom's face popped out. "This is your room, up on the second floor. I put your bags at the foot of your bed. Waylon's just down the hall from you. I called the queen. I forgot, she had a hair appointment in town. She'll be back soon."

Celia and I were grateful to have a moment to settle into the house before meeting Nadia. And upon her arrival some thirty minutes later, Nadia said that yes, she thought her American brother and sister would appreciate a minute to themselves following the car trip. Then she extended her fingers long below her round face and said, "What do you think of my hair? I went blonde with black roots and had them take off six inches. I feel like a leopard who's lost her spots."

Nadia was striking no matter the length or color of her hair. She had cut it very short, within two inches of the scalp. She wasn't tall, even in the suede high heels she was now sliding out of. She had narrow Slavic eyes and crooked teeth but a powerfully affecting smile, which she had already flashed several times since coming into the house.

"So, how are my Americans?" she said, taking her hands through her hair and seeming to enjoy the feel of the new, fresh cut. "Tired? Hungry? Thirsty? You know, I don't drink anymore, never even a drop, but there's a whole wine cellar down in the basement with bottles and bottles of great wine. You should drink as much of it as you like. Dom. Dom."

Dom had been in the bathroom, hiding perhaps. This, at least, had been Nadia's impression.

"Get out here. Don't malinger," said Nadia, snapping her fingers. "Dom, go to the wine cellar and bring back a bottle of red wine for your countryman and woman."

"Do I have to?" said Dom.

"Yes. You must."

Nadia rolled her dark eyes at us and then began to unload some of the fresh vegetables from a sack she'd set down on the long wooden kitchen counter. She said she would send Dom back to Detroit—pronounced it *Deeee-troy-t*—if the young assistant continued to behave so brazenly.

"As they say, good help is just so hard to find. This is why I'm so glad you have come, Celia." Nadia stepped back from the counter and took Celia by the shoulders. "Paul, don't worry," she said, "I won't steal her. But what an extraordinary painter, so skilled—to have you in the studio will be my honor and privilege."

Celia quietly began to laugh.

"What? What? You think I'm being funny? Paul," said Nadia, "do you think I'm joking?"

"I don't."

"Well, I'm not." But Nadia was laughing too now. "Ah, my Americans, my American family, we're going to have a very good time. But where is the little one? Oh, Little One. Little One. I don't see him. Does he like his room? It's little Jan's room when he's here with his father, Karl, my boyfriend.

It's too bad the boys aren't here to meet you. Jan and Waylon would get along so well. But who knows, maybe they'll come over the weekend. You would love Karl, Paul. He's also a writer. Have you seen his writing studio yet?"

"No."

"My God, well let me show you where you'll do your work while you're here. It is almost as beautiful a studio as my own."

Nadia led us out a back door. A short footbridge over a stream separated the writer's studio from the house. The grass was high and unattended. The sound of our shoes cutting through the green blades competed with the hum of insects. The writing studio resembled a Scandinavian log cabin with long tree trunk beams stacked one on top of the other and crossing at the corners. Nadia pushed open the front door and first things first, she instructed everyone to shut their eyes and take a deep breath.

"You, too, my little American," she said to Waylon.

No one, not even Waylon, failed to remark on just how wonderful the wood smelled.

"Isn't it glorious?" said Nadia. "Sometimes I come here just to breathe in the aroma."

Six bookcases stretched to the ceiling, a few thousand books, their spines organized by color. Nadia asked me what I thought of them. "Aren't they beautiful? I bought each and every one for Karl, the love of my life."

"It's a great collection," I said.

"Yes, but they're in Polish, so, they won't mean anything to you."

"Not true. They already mean so much, Nadia. Just to be surrounded by them makes my heart beat faster."

"If you take one off the shelf, please put it back where you found it. Karl can be a monster about his books."

Next, Nadia took us over to the art studio. Like a rectory to a cathedral, so the writing studio compared to Nadia's art studio. The ceilings were four times higher, the windows twice as large. Sunlight exploded into the room. I noticed one, two, three, four—ten—canvases, each one of them over six feet tall by four feet wide, give or take, hanging from the studio walls, one beside the other, with only the underpaintings complete.

"Are these the paintings Celia will be working on?" I asked.

"Yes," said, Nadia. "We start this afternoon."

A moment later, out in the field, with Waylon and Nadia holding hands some twenty paces ahead, I said to Celia, "Good lord, that's a whole lot of work ahead of you."

"I know," she said. "I knew it would be. It's what I signed up for. But it's okay, because I'm doing it for us—for you, for me, and Waylon."

"Thank you, my love. Thank you a million times over."

An hour later, Celia had gone off with Nadia to the art studio. With Waylon asleep in his bed, I slipped down the hall to the bedroom where Celia and I would be staying, an average-sized room with a skylight above a queen bed, a dresser, a small armoire and a desk. All of a sudden, I heard my name being called.

"Paul. Hey, Paul!"

It was Dom at the bottom of the staircase.

"What is it, Dom?" I leaned over the railing. Dom had shaving cream on her cheeks, her long blonde hair was tucked under a gray fedora, and the rest of her was buttoned into a black suit. I said, "Why are you all dressed up?"

"I need your help."

"With what?"

"I'm shooting a self-portrait. Can you come here for a second?"

I drew one hand down the middle of my face, sighing, and went downstairs to the kitchen. Dom had a straight edge razor and a bowl of water, a dish of shaving soap, and a shaving brush on the dining table beside a vase of purple and yellow tulips. At the foot of the table an old Pentax was set up on a tripod. Dom, sitting down at the dining table, lifting her chin and reapplying the shaving cream, said, "Okay, you're going to start shooting photos. Don't stop, all right? Keep shooting."

I took one photo after another while Dom dipped the brush in the water, made slow circles with its quills in the dish of shaving soap, and then lathered up her face. She then began to shave her face. She started with the left side, close to the earlobe, worked her way down toward her chin and the space above the upper lip. Dom removed the fedora now and shook out her hair. I could see that she had cut herself not once or twice but many times, her blood mixing with the shaving soap and forming a haunting swirl of whites and reds.

"It looks great," I said.

Dom brought a towel to her face, cleaning off the shaving soap and blood. Gazing up at me, she said, "Thanks for saying, Paul. But I already knew it would."

16

Appetites

Nadia and Celia came in from the art studio just minutes before dinner, both in good spirits. Dom and I had polished off over half a liter of vodka and were doing quite well ourselves.

"Would you like a drink?" I said to Nadia.

"No, no, I've given it up," she said.

"I'm so sorry. You already told us that."

"Oh no, don't be sorry," said Nadia. "I forget sometimes myself."

"Where's Waylon?" said Celia. Her hands had only a little paint on them. She was a very neat painter, Celia, precise and neat. I had never once seen her emerge from the studio looking like some abstract expressionist after a war with a few gallons of paint.

"Hopefully upstairs in his bed. I'll go check." I stood up, teetering. "I'll be back."

The child was still asleep. Though exhausted myself, I reckoned that it would be rude to turn in now. It was the first night in Rabka—our first meal with Nadia—and I had to take part and show my host some respect. It was only ten after eight, besides. I should stay up and continue to adjust to the new time zone.

When I returned to the dining table, Nadia, Dom, and Celia were all laughing.

"My Dominika is like a wild animal," said Nadia. "You have to be firm with her or she'll claw out your eyes. Some days we have to give her a big cut of steak. She has such an appetite," Nadia howled.

"Speaking of appetites, I'm famished," said Celia.

"Let's eat," said Nadia. Dom had prepared the dinner, chicken and vegetables and potatoes, which sat in large serving bowls on the kitchen counter. "Quickly, Celia, help yourself before Dom devours it all. She's a beast, so hungry for meat. Beware, any kind will do."

"Okay, all right," said Dom. The suit jacket was off. She was wearing a floral apron over her clothes. "I'm not amused. Everyone give your attention over to your stomachs and let's stop discussing mine."

After dinner, Celia and I retired for the night. Celia wanted a good night's rest ahead of a long day of painting, and I had to wake at dawn and work before anyone else was up. I checked on Waylon one last time before shutting ourselves into our bedroom. At one moment, we were discussing how tired we were, but at the next we were having sex. Lying in each other's arms afterward, Celia said:

"I'm so happy."

"Me, too."

"Come closer," she said, "as close as you can."

We pressed our bodies together as tight as we could and eventually fell asleep, clinging to one another.

My alarm clock went off at 5:00 a.m., and I shot out of bed. Walking through the grass with my laptop under my arm, a mug of hot coffee in my hand and only the moonlight to brighten my path, I saw the writing studio straight ahead of me. I threw open the door and flipped on a light. Now I would really look at this room. It was a beauty, with a harmony there between the large picture windows and the wood and the books, the thousands of books. I had to turn a cursed corner in by later this morning, but I had my notes with plenty of corners to choose from and more than enough time and the sort of peace and quiet with which to write that I almost never had at the apartment in Brooklyn.

"Paul, my dear sweet American."

I swung around on the chair, spilling hot coffee in my lap. Nadia lay on a daybed in the corner of the room, the shadows obscuring her all this time.

"You scared the shit out of me."

"What are you doing awake?" she said. Her head was still on the pillow. She looked as if she'd been crying.

"I came in here to work. It's the only time I have. I've got to be with Waylon while Celia's in the studio with you. What are *you* doing here? I thought your bedroom was down the hall from ours."

Her eyes were dark and sad but trying to conjure some kind of happiness. She said, "I've been up all night. I lost patience with my empty bed and came in here to breathe in the smell of the wood."

"Well, yes, it really does smell good in here."

"Oh, Paul—Karl is giving me such trouble."

"Who?"

"My boyfriend, Karl. You're a man and a father, like Karl. You'll give me some advice?"

"Oh, sure, Nadia. You're free to tell me anything you like. I'll certainly let you know what I think if that's what you want."

"I do. Desperately. You see, Karl, he's been avoiding me. He doesn't want to be around me. He won't come here, for instance. Maybe he just needs time away."

"Do *you* think he does?"

"I don't know, Paul. Maybe," she said. "I just don't want to have to beg for him to love me back."

"I understand that," I said.

"I *love* Karl. I love his son. I think of myself as like a mother to the child. The three of us are a family. I bought Karl all these books. I didn't have to. I mean, he isn't poor. He comes from money. But I like to buy people gifts, especially the people I love."

"It seems to me that your lives are very intertwined. You have a bedroom here for his son. That means a lot."

"It does though, doesn't it? I love that child as if he were my own."

"Ideally, would you and Karl marry?"

"Yes," said Nadia, "but I don't think Karl would marry me."

"Why do you say that?"

"Because, *because* it is so complicated, Paul."

The sun was starting to rise, and I could hear birds chirping. At the risk of insulting Nadia, I said, "I'm sorry, but I really have to work. Maybe I'll just go back inside the house and—"

"No, no, no, please stay with me, Paul. Don't leave." Nadia stared at me, tears falling from her eyes. "I'm too sad to be left alone."

"Nadia, I have a deadline."

"Please, Paul. Don't go."

No doubt a measure of defense against my leaving her, Nadia began telling me how difficult it was to be in a relationship with Karl and how lucky I was to have Celia. She began sobbing.

"I'm sorry, Nadia. Don't cry, please. It's okay."

"Oh, Paul," she said, "it hurts me so. I just want to have what *you* have."

"Well, thank you, but—"

"Your family is perfect, Paul. Oh, how, Paul, *how* do I get a perfect family of my own? Oh, Paul, *Paul*," she said, weeping more and more. "Please, tell me, help me, direct me. I am your student now. You are the teacher. Teach me, please."

"I don't have the answers, Nadia."

"Stop saying that!" Nadia smacked me in the shoulder. She said, "I see your family. I see what you have. You know *something*, Paul."

"No. I don't know anything."

"But you *do* know something. You must. Look at what you have!"

Our conversation went on like this for twenty more minutes. Longer, maybe. At last, Nadia calmed down, curled up on the daybed, closed her eyes, and fell asleep. I went back into the house and considered working at the kitchen table, but Nadia had taken something vital from me, stolen it, and I decided to do something I rarely ever did: rerun an old cursed corner, this one on the Beekman Tower. Then I got back into bed and passed out next to Celia.

17

To Manage Expectations

Nadia was still asleep around 1:00 p.m. Dom said the best thing to do was to let her rest. As for Celia, she and Nadia had already discussed the work. Nadia's painting needs were with the human form. In each painting, Nadia would have a structure in the background, a home like the one here in Rabka, but maybe a slick glass apartment sky-rise or a Soviet-era government building. In the foreground, always, a model-beautiful woman in stylish outfits would be striking a serious pose. Though Nadia conceived of these great compositions, she wasn't a master with the human form. Her paintings had an unintentional lifelessness to them. Enter: Celia.

That morning, while Celia worked in the art studio, Waylon and I lounged in a kiddie pool in the middle of the grass field behind the house. Dom lay nearby on a chaise in a pair of black leather pants and no top, sunning herself. At some point, we heard a wild shriek echo out across the land, and Nadia came running. Her face was red and sweaty. She was whelping in a frenzy of sorts.

"Karl and Jan are coming out tonight! Karl and Jan are coming out tonight!" she was screaming.

"Oh, yeah? That's terrific," I said. "What did you tell him?"

"I said that I would donate all his books to the local library if he didn't come out here right away. *And now?* Now he's driving over in just a few hours." She kissed me on the forehead. "He's promised to spend the whole week here. Thank you, Paul. You are very good with relationship-advice."

"I don't remember telling you to threaten Karl."

"Oh, but you give very good advice. You do."

Nadia sprang into full preparation mode. Karl would be in Rabka tonight—his son, Jan, too—and Nadia would make sure to load the house with every kind of provision. She went to the market in town, taking Dom along to help. Upon their return, the house looked like Christmas, with gift-wrapped boxes, bottles of champagne, a large tin of caviar, and exotic cheeses and clementines spilled out across the dining table. I wondered if Karl wouldn't consider these efforts suffocating, whether Nadia shouldn't be more modest and easy going considering the distance Karl had been keeping. Presently, Nadia was rubbing down a whole chicken with a garlic clove and shouting at Dom to clean and peel the potatoes already and quit wasting time.

I'd been given my own assignments. I mowed the lawn and was then handed a broom by Nadia and told to sweep all the floors, upstairs and downstairs. Minutes after, Nadia's phone rang and she excused herself, for Karl was calling. She disappeared into the office beside the front door entrance, beneath the stairs leading up to the second floor.

Dom propped her feet up on the dining table and lit a cigarette. "This isn't good."

"You think he's backing out?" I asked.

Dom didn't answer, didn't have to. The office was some thirty feet from the kitchen and though Nadia had shut the door behind her, we could all hear her screaming on the phone in Polish.

Dom asked me if I'd like her to translate.

"Better not," I said, "what with Waylon sitting here."

"Wise." Dom swung her feet to the floor, stood, and announced, "I'm going off to hide. I advise you all to do the same. Things *will* get worse from here."

An hour later, Celia came in from the studio and wasn't too far gone from an intense seven hour stretch of painting not to notice that something was off. Nevertheless, she wasn't ready to hear about it. She had to shower.

It seemed we wouldn't all have dinner together, that Nadia would remain on the phone arguing with Karl and that Dom would stay in her bedroom and that Celia would not return from the shower. Then, after another thirty minutes, Nadia began shouting from the bottom of the staircase for everyone to come down and eat—"Let's go, dinner's served! Let's go. Let's go. Dinner!"—and one by one, everyone reappeared.

In times like these, children could be especially useful. Of course, Waylon had no idea what was going on between Nadia and Karl, and unlike the others, he remained talkative and silly. He giggled and played with his food. Normally his parents would tell him not to, but his potato sculpture was perhaps the only thing standing between Nadia and a breakdown. Unfortunately, the child was just buying us time, only delaying the inevitable.

"I want to kill him. Kill. Him. He torments me. It's all a game. He is a sick person. *Sick*, I tell you."

No one dared speak a word. Nadia didn't want to hear from anyone, anyway.

"I want to give him all of my love, and he rejects me. So, why do I keep trying to get him to love me back? Why? I am a human being. I have limits. I can only take so much pain and suffering."

Nadia sat at the head of the table, an empty seat reserved for Karl to her left and one for Jan to her right. She was covering her face with her hands. Waylon slipped out of his chair and went to where Nadia was slumped over the table, and he placed his hand on her shoulder.

"It's okay," said Waylon, patting Nadia on the back.

Nadia wiped her eyes and hugged the boy. "Thank you, my little friend. Thank you so much. Your auntie Nadia is grateful. Come. Let's eat this beautiful meal and forget our troubles. Pour me a little champagne, Dom, would you?"

"Are you sure?" said Dom.

"Yes, yes. Just two fingers. No more."

Dom filled a champagne flute halfway. Nadia hardly drank any. She seemed to like holding the glass, looking at it. Every so often she would touch the champagne to her lips. In time, however, the dinner party moved outdoors behind the house, and Nadia was skipping across the grass, pretending to flap imaginary wings. Waylon chased after her but could not catch up.

"Tweet-tweet-tweet," she said, lifting her knees up high. "I'm a bird. Tweet-tweet-tweet."

Celia, Dom, and I were laughing but weren't so much amused as concerned for Nadia. There was an unspoken hope that her performance would end soon.

"Oh my God, I've had an...*ep...ep...epiphany*" said Nadia, suddenly. Her hands moved to her head and with her eyes wide, she said, "Celia, I...I want you to paint a portrait of Dom. I *want* a portrait of Dom, a great big nude. I'll pay you for it. Let's go right now. Come on, everyone to the studio."

We all froze, save for Waylon who was pulling on Nadia, trying to get her attention.

"Nadia, please," said Celia, "you don't really mean it."

"Even if she does," said Dom, "it's not happening."

Nadia clapped her hands together belligerently. One sip of champagne was all it had taken to put her in this state. I knew others like this: the smallest amount of alcohol and a switch went off in them. She was saying, "I want it, I want it, I want it. I'll pay you both. Dom for your time and your body, you get five thousand dollars. And Celia, for your genius, you get fifteen. *No,* twenty!"

Celia drew her hair back in her hands so that the cool air could touch her neck. She said, "Nadia, please. I'm here to paint *your* work."

"That's right, you are. But I am in the presence of one of the great painters of the human form," said Nadia, stomping her feet in the grass, "and I will not waste this opportunity to have one of your portraits for myself. Now, to the studio! Come on, everyone. Right now."

"You know, we have to put Waylon to bed," I said.

"*You* put Waylon to bed," said Nadia, flipping a hand at me. "I'm taking Celia with me. Bye-bye. Go along now, Paul."

Celia shot me a look. "It's okay," she said. "Just go. I'll handle this."

"Nadia," I said, "you should really—"

"Paul, just take Waylon up to bed," said Celia. "It's okay."

I picked up Waylon and walked back into the house. Tempering my anger, I changed him into his pajamas. We brushed our teeth. Then Waylon begged to sleep in the bed with me. I agreed. Waylon was out after twenty minutes, but I lay there for an hour attending to my anger. I told myself that none of this mattered. Nadia couldn't handle alcohol. This was why she didn't drink it. And then, either way, she wouldn't remember any of this tomorrow. None of it would mean anything to her. There was no reason to carry these feelings with me any further.

"Just let it go," I said. "Just sleep."

And I did, at least for a while. In the middle of the night, I woke. I looked around for Celia, but she wasn't in the bed with me. I rose to my feet, saw the light on in the hallway, heard music and voices. I checked the time on my phone. It was 4:15 in the morning. I couldn't believe they were all still up.

I went back to bed.

18

In the Woods

Waylon and I slept in until nine o'clock. Celia was back in the bed by then, but neither she nor Nadia nor Dom were up. I made us scrambled eggs and toast, and then we went for a walk around the woods. Next, we greeted the neighbor's cows, standing behind a wooden fence and calling to them with our *moooos*. The air was cool, clean, and soothing, and I took it in in deep, satisfying breaths. When Waylon bored of this, he took off in the direction of the art studio, and I followed after him. I was surprised to see the sliding glass door of the studio had been left slightly ajar. I went to close it.

"Dad!"

"Hold on."

"Dad!"

"I said hold on, Waylon!"

Up on the wall farthest from the door, at a distance of some thirty feet, I noticed a new painting, of Dom. A simple nude, life-size, something Celia had clearly made very fast, with big brush strokes and not a lot of detail—my chest hurt now. This painting, I hated it; I couldn't believe Celia had even made it. Why would she? Not for money. No, she wouldn't be paid anything for it. Celia, awake in bed now, eyes puffy, skin splotchy, a frog in her throat, was telling me that it was a gift from her to Nadia.

"A gift for Nadia?"

"That's right," said Celia.

"You're making Nadia gifts of your paintings now?"

"Of the one, yes."

But Celia held up a hand and asked me not to speak. Nadia was texting her and Dom from her bedroom. Celia read the text aloud: she could get to the studio by two; Dom should go buy provisions from the store in town and prepare a lunch.

"I should really help Dom with the shopping. I'll be back in thirty minutes," said Celia, and she threw on her white dress and shot out the door and into the car with Dom. A dark feeling rose up in me. The vision of Celia in motion, the speed with which her body moved—I knew the meaning of this energy.

I figured Celia's presence would knock the feeling out of me, that being in her company, in our usual manner, would free me of it. Back home, she and Dom sorted through the groceries together, putting away most of what they had bought and keeping on the kitchen counter what they planned to use for lunch. All the while their hands passed over each other's shoulders and elbows—all this light touching right in front of me, while I played Go Fish with Waylon at the dining table. Celia laughed generously every time Dom said anything at all. Slicing tomatoes at the kitchen counter, Dom came up behind Celia and set her hand on her lower back, left it there. She complimented Celia on her knife work, something which Celia thought was hysterically funny. She told Dom that she better be careful, that as it concerned sharp objects, she could be deadly.

"Dad, your turn."

"What?"

"It's *your* turn," said Waylon.

"Yes. Sorry. Here I go."

After lunch, Celia went up to the painting studio to work. Dom insisted on cleaning the kitchen and recruited Waylon to be her helper. She assured me that she didn't mind watching him, that I could go off and do as I liked for the next few hours. Waylon seemed pleased by the prospect of an afternoon with Dom, and so I went to the writing studio. Crossing over the footbridge through the tall grass, I acknowledged that to look after Celia's child, to seek closeness through a connection with Waylon—yes, she must be experiencing a deep feeling for Celia. But I didn't care right now. It was a quarter after two and I had been handed some hours of free time.

I sat at the desk in the writing studio, but I couldn't work. Staring out through the large window, I saw Dom and Waylon crossing the lawn to the art studio and the vision of her aroused the same dark bodily feeling as before. I shot to my feet, pacing for a long while. Around four o'clock, Nadia paid me a visit. Wrapped in a white sheet, with only her head exposed, she curled up beside my chair and put her head on my knee, shutting her eyes.

"How are you, Paul?"

"I'm busy," I said. "I have to work. I have a deadline. You have to leave me alone."

"Are you writing about me, your Polish sister?"

"No, I am not writing about you."

"But we keep it very interesting around here, don't we?"

"It depends on what one's interests are, Nadia, now doesn't it?"

Nadia locked her arms around my ankle, brought her cheek flat against my thigh. "I had a very difficult time yesterday. I'm sorry. Thank you for being my friend. Thank you for caring about me. You give the best advice. Really, the best, Paul. Is your column about giving love-advice?"

"No, Nadia." I sighed. This was hopeless. "And it's a newsletter, not a column."

"What's your newsletter about?" she wanted to know. "Is it about travel? Are you a travel writer?"

"Nadia, I really can't right now. Listen, I know you went through a lot last night. I'm glad that everyone could be there for you and—"

"Oh, Paul, I wouldn't have been able to live through such a night without the support of all of you. I want to show my appreciation. We should have a small party tonight in your honor."

"That's not necessary, Nadia."

Nadia tightened around my leg, said, "But I want to celebrate."

"Maybe we take a night off and celebrate tomorrow."

Nadia lifted her head, her eyes locking with mine. "There's no reason to wait. I have two friends already coming over tonight. One is the editor of *Polish Vogue* and the other is her assistant editor. We should show them a great time, a big celebration."

"Two editors from *Polish Vogue* are coming over tonight?"

"Yes," said Nadia, "and we have much to do. Yesterday's preparations for Karl will seem like nothing compared to what we'll be serving up tonight. This evening will be spectacular. It has to be."

"Okay," I said. And now I was up on my feet.

"Where are you going? Don't run away from me."

"I am not *running away* from you. I'm going to check on my son."

I found Waylon asleep in his bed and got in next to him. What was this exhaustion? It began at my heart and moved through me, down to my toes. I passed out and was awoken sometime later by Celia, who slid in naked under the covers. She had just taken a shower, her skin and hair damp. She brought an arm over me and Waylon.

"How are my fellas?"

"Sleeping," I said.

Out the bedroom window, I could see the sun setting in the sky. The air was warm, thick.

"Did you know we have guests coming tonight?" said Celia. "*Polish Vogue.*"

"I want a night off."

"You won't have to do much," she said. "I'll help Dom and Nadia. You can hang out with Waylon."

"Oh, can I?" I said. "You'll allow for that?"

"What's gotten into you?"

"Nothing," I said.

"Doesn't *seem* like nothing, Paul. Is there something you want to say?"

"Is there something *you* want to say?"

"No. There isn't."

"You're sure?"

We stared at one another for one, two, three seconds—and then Celia walked off.

By seven o'clock, the house was in full swing, busy. Salmon steaks baked in the oven, their aroma strong even upstairs on the second floor. Greens were brought in from the garden and being painstakingly washed by Dom at the kitchen sink. If a speck of dirt or an insect were discovered on a leaf of lettuce, the assistant would be walking back to Krakow, said Nadia. Champagne was put on ice, vodka was chilling in the freezer, wine was coming up from the cellar. Nadia was assembling floral arrangements for the entryway and the outdoor dining table. The night air and the expanse of grass and the farmland in the distance and the darkening sky seemed loaded up with the promise of a special evening ahead. There was beauty, and plenty of it, and it all brought about a deepened sense of possibility.

Waylon and I were in charge of setting the table, though my son didn't assist so much as tumble around the grass and chase after butterflies. Celia came walking out the side door in a brown stretchy cotton dress, the material trailing behind her as she circled the dining table. She moved right past me, ignoring my look, and scooped up Waylon, squeezing him.

"Hi, my perfect American family," said Nadia, appearing suddenly at her second-floor bedroom window. "You all look beautiful. If I could ever have a family that looks like yours and loves like you do, I would be the happiest woman on the planet. Ach, it will never happen. But tonight we will have fun, I know it."

Nadia told us she had to get ready now and that she would be down as quickly as she possibly could, but should the *Vogue* editors arrive to please make them feel at home. Dom joined us after a few minutes, declaring that every dinner preparation had been made. She lowered herself into a chair, lighting a cigarette. She gave Celia a look then.

"Would you like a drink?" Celia asked her.

"That'd be great."

"Vodka soda?"

"Please," said Dom.

Dom watched Celia walk into the house, her attention then traveling up to the sky. She slid down low in the chair, exhaling smoke.

Celia returned with Dom's drink. The dull, dark feeling announced itself again. I held no drink, Celia hadn't thought to offer me one. I went inside and fixed one: a tall vodka on ice. I was halfway finished and about to fill it again when the doorbell rang.

"Someone get it, please!" shouted Nadia from upstairs. "I need five more minutes."

A tall blonde in high heels and a dark-haired woman in flats smiled and waved at me from behind the screen door at the entry.

"Hello, hello," I said, letting them in. "I'm Paul. How are you? Welcome. I'm a friend of Nadia's. She'll be down soon. Have you come from Krakow? How was the traffic? You must want a drink."

They did.

"Do vodka sodas work? Excellent. Good. I'll bring two outside. You go and sit down," I said. "Yes, right through those doors there."

I headed for the kitchen again while the *Vogue* editors went out to join Celia and Dom. Admittedly, I was pleased to have these women here. I could flirt with them, I could antagonize Celia—as she was antagonizing me with Dom—especially once we all sat for dinner. But then throughout the meal, with Celia and Dom seated next to one another, their pleasure apparent, I found it more and more difficult to speak at all. I imagined these two Polish women found my silence unattractive. Had I no charisma? No charm? Dom, who was in total control of herself, a lively, witty participant, was stealing my powers, it seemed. Not even Nadia bossing Dom around diminished her presence. When Nadia ordered her into the kitchen to bring out the salmon steaks and salad, Dom answered, "Yes, milady," and caused the whole table to laugh and ridicule Nadia for being too demanding.

"I pay her twice what she's worth," said Nadia, in her own defense.

"And I would serve her majesty for no money at all," said Dom. "It is my honor to do so."

Nadia threw her hands up and said, "Well, there you have it. I *am* a queen. Be sure to say so in the magazine."

"But of course," said the brunette.

Her name was Marta. The blonde was Anja. Their full attention was on Nadia. This was a business dinner, they were getting a story, and no one at the table but Nadia mattered to them. That is, I didn't stand a chance with either. As for Celia and Dom, I couldn't come between them now. But I could let go. I would start...*now*. I poured myself another vodka and by the time dinner was finished, I did feel looser. I was able to speak. I could laugh, too. The dull, dark feeling hadn't lifted—it was there with me—but the vodka did something to hold it at bay. After dessert, I put Waylon to bed. It would have been easy for me to fall asleep next to him while everyone else went up to the art studio to see the paintings.

I got up and rejoined the others at the outdoor dining table, which had been cleared, save for the metal buckets for the champagne, the vodka, and the wine. Celia and Dom weren't at the table with the others, hadn't made it back from the studio. Nadia was talking to Marta and Anja in Polish—I couldn't understand them—and then she brought out the painting of Dom that Celia had made last night, leaned it right against the outdoor table. A portrait, so simple and strong—that's what Nadia, Marta, and Anja were saying now in English. There was a sexuality to it that could hardly be contained by the canvas.

"It's fucking hot," said Nadia. "Don't you think?"

"It is," said Marta.

"I am in love with it," said Anja. "There is so much pulsing sexuality."

"Paul, what do you think of the painting?" said Nadia. "It turns you on, doesn't it?"

Where were Dom and Celia? I would kill them both.

I got up from the table. Dizzy from the vodka, I went into the house. I checked the kitchen, the pantry, the office at the front of the house. My blood was charged, my heart thrusting in my chest. I looked in all the bedrooms and then did a loop of the house from the outside. Ready to go up to the art studio, I heard voices coming through the window of the bathroom on the first floor, the sound of whispers carrying in the night air. I went straight inside the house and threw open the bathroom door.

Celia and Dom were on top of each other, leaning into a wall, their shirts off.

"Get the fuck out of here, right now!" I screamed at Dom. She held her hands up over her head. "Go! Get the fuck out of here, now!"

"I'm sorry," she said, shirking away. "Celia told me you wouldn't care."

"Fuck off!" And then, to Celia: "You are such a shit!"

Her mouth was red, the blood vessels still pulsing from where Dom's lips had just been. She said, "I'm sorry. Don't kill Dom. I told her you wouldn't mind."

"Well, fuck you! Fuck you, Celia. How could you do this!" I started to walk away, outside, into the woods. I said, "Don't follow me, Celia. Stay away. I'm serious!"

"I'm sorry, my love, please. I'm really so sorry." She was crying, drunk. She trailed me through the trees.

"I said stay away. You have no heart. You're cruel."

"I'm sorry, I'm so, so sorry, *please*."

"Why would you do this to me? How could you!"

"I'm sorry. I love you. Please forgive me."

"No," I said, screaming out in the dark woods. Then I collapsed with what felt like my full weight against a tree, head to forearm. "I can't believe it. I can't believe I ever came to this fucking place, Celia. I'm so stupid."

"Please, Paul. It was nothing. It didn't mean anything, I swear."

"But it does. I'm trying to bring us closer to each other and you…you…"

"I know, Paul, and I'm sorry."

"No, no, no, you're not—you're not sorry."

"I *am*." She was pulling me to turn and face her. "I swear, it didn't mean a thing. I was just having fun."

And then in the darkness, between trees, Celia threw me to the ground, opened my pants, lifted her dress, and fucked me.

PART 4

19
Paint

We didn't talk about Poland. Not a single word. No one even alluded to it, not once. Instead, we got a new apartment.

The new apartment.

Almost nothing that had belonged to Celia and Graham came with us. We moved ten blocks away into an apartment half the size of the old one and bought all-new everything. New furniture, new mugs with new catchphrases, new plates and silverware, new pots and pans, new candlestick holders, new trashcans, even a new toilet brush and plunger, and all with Celia's paycheck from Poland. I tried to ignore this fact, but then I would lie down on the new bed and think about how it was no better than the bed before it, the one that had belonged to Celia and Graham, because of Poland. The same was true of all the new furniture, the knickknacks: the jar in the bathroom that held our three toothbrushes, the bronze dish by the door where we tossed our keys and loose change, the rug at the foot of the bed. I could not *unsee* Poland in these things, could not rid my mind of the image of Celia and Dom in the bathroom with their hands all over one another's half-naked bodies.

"Do you love the apartment? Is it everything you wanted?" asked Celia.

We were painting the trim of Waylon's bedroom doorway a canary yellow, one of the many flourishes being applied to the apartment. Celia had so many ideas for how to make our new home beautiful: wallpapering our bedroom a handsome, lush green; swapping out the cheap brass doorknobs for colored glass knobs; buying ornate fabrics for use as window curtains and upholstery for our new dining room chairs.

She dipped a paintbrush into the small jar of paint, smiling at me. "Is there anything you think we should add to our home?"

"Something else? What more could we need?"

"I don't know," she said. "It's why I'm asking you. This is *our* home. I want you to feel that your stamp is on it. But I've picked out everything and made all the decisions about the decor."

"I prefer it that way. You've got the better taste between us, Celia. You know how things should be."

"Well, what about the color for the kitchen?"

The canary yellow was perfect for the trim of Waylon's doorway, bright and joyful. I told her so, adding, "You have the professional's sense of color."

"Yes, but I want to know what you think about the color for the kitchen, Paul?"

"I really can't talk about paint anymore. What are we even talking about, anyway?"

"What do you mean by that?"

"I mean, what are we *talking* about, Celia?"

"Paint, Paul—we're talking about paint."

She stared at me, stoical, unphased, the paintbrush held at an angle beside her brown, placid eyes.

We painted the kitchen off-white—but then two weeks later, it all came out. We were at the same East Village sushi bar where Celia had asked me about monogamy and whether I thought it possible for two people to stay faithful to one another forever when she told me she had met a woman and wanted to start seeing her *openly*. This was new for us, and how did I feel about the idea? Was I for or against it?

I pointed at my sake glass. Celia took the carafe, refilled it. I threw back the shot of sake and said, "I think it's a great idea, Celia."

"You do? Really? Because there's a woman I'm interested in dating."

"Good. I'm sure there is."

"And you can see anyone you like."

"Perfect."

"You're really open to this, Paul? I'm being serious."

"You'd better be. This is serious stuff, Celia."

"All right then. Good. I'm happy to hear you say so."

I assumed the woman Celia had in mind was Anne Noel, but according to Celia there had never been a romance there. Anne was a friend, an honest wife, devoted to her husband and to her home. Moreover, she didn't like to complicate her life in any way whatsoever. She also lacked the ability to plan ahead: essential for having an affair, apparently. Indeed, for Anne, choosing a day and time to do anything was impossible—hence, the last-minute trip to Paris.

I sat listening to Celia, chopsticks in hand, itchy under the collar, warm, losing strength. I wanted to believe everything she was saying. Yes, Anne was just a friend. No, there had never been anything funny between them. Celia had just said so.

How relieving.

But Celia wasn't here to talk about Anne. The reason for this conversation about *opening* our relationship concerned someone else entirely, and that person was Dom.

"But she's in Poland, isn't she?"

"Not anymore. She's moved to New York."

"Well, that's a fucking ridiculous decision, don't you think? That she would come all the way here, being that you're in a relationship with me and that we have a family and—"

"Paul, don't shout at me. Let me speak. I want to tell you everything."

"Another bottle of sake!" I yelled to the waitress.

Celia had emailed Dom soon after we flew home and they started communicating daily. Celia had convinced herself this was the best kind of relationship for her, beyond the one she shared with me. Dom was an eight-hour plane ride away and there was no possibility of seeing her and complicating her life. But in short time Dom brought up the idea of coming back to the United States to live. She lacked purpose in Poland, New York would offer her real possibilities, she didn't want to work for Nadia anymore, and so on. Celia would never discourage Dom from moving to New York. Nor could she deny how much she wanted her close by. After our return from Poland, Celia had begun to feel that same loss of direction, and the new apartment had been an attempt to find one, she admitted now. Celia had put herself to making our new home as wonderful a place as she could, but that project had resolved nothing for her. She did not want *this* life. Then she began to talk to Dom every day and those disturbances of the heart began to recede. As for her painting, Celia said she had felt stuck for years, struggling to figure out what, if anything, she had to say. But she had been greatly inspired by the painting of Dom, and she started to make more works of her, using screenshots. Right away she knew she had a subject, *a voice*. Celia said there was a vividness to the paintings, a strong beating pulse that had been missing from her work for years. The paintings were overtly sexual in nature.

"I had no idea you had been making new portraits of Dom."

"The canvases are small. I've been hiding them from you. I wasn't sure you'd want to see them," she said. "Do you?"

"Maybe. I don't know."

I wasn't sure that I did. Not that it would matter for long. The paintings of Dom had attracted the attention of a very good Chelsea gallery. Celia had been invited to participate in a group show a few months from now. The show would be a big step forward for her. The gallery had even suggested that they might be interested in a solo show next year.

"It's what I've been working toward all these years. I'm sorry that it's happening this way, but this is the reality."

"That's incredible," I said, suddenly sober, subdued. "And it's okay, I'm a great fan of reality."

"And you really think it's a good idea?"

"Of us both seeing other women?"

"Yes. Tell me the truth, do you really like this idea?"

I understood that Celia wasn't asking my permission. She would do it either way.

"Okay," I said, "let's try it out."

"Well, that's great. Thank you, baby. Thank you," she said, squeezing my hand, kissing the knuckles. "*So*, tell me, who are you going to go out with first?"

20

Other Women

I invited Leah to my uncle's beach apartment in Westhampton, the same place Celia and I used to go when she was married to Graham. Our first morning there, Leah and I went clamming in the bay. We wore rubber waders that came up to our ribs, the bay floor mucky and warm with jagged parts. I used a rake to free shells from the sludge below. Leah, her long blonde hair up above light, concentrating eyes, tallied the number of clams in the shiny metal bucket in her arms. Flies swarmed near the bay's black, reflective surface. In the distance we heard a tennis ball being swatted back and forth over a net. A man was windsurfing, and the sun had yet to rise very high in the sky. Upstairs, I changed into a white bathrobe, steamed the clams, and then scrambled them with eggs and shallots. Leah squeezed tangerines and opened a bottle of champagne for mimosas. On the porch, facing the ocean, we sat with our breakfast and drinks before us. I leaned over and kissed a bony point of Leah's shoulder. She pressed her hand to my cheek.

"It's wonderful here," she said.

"Isn't it, though?"

I told her about the Surf and Sands. Constructed in the 1920s, the apartment had been in my family since after the Second World War. It was one of thirty-two small identical side-by-side units with a room on the beach and a second room facing the bay. The tenants, most of whom were old and had been coming here for a very long time, still remembered all the hurricanes and the shark attacks, the heatwaves, the beached whales, and the beginning of what they called the "piping plover invasion." Back when Celia and I would come here, we would run from those diving birds, the two of us holding hands, our feet kicking up hot sand. I did not tell Leah that part. I had been careful not to mention Celia's name even once.

After breakfast we sunbathed a short distance from where the tide came in and the sand became an escarpment. Seagulls circled the ocean. A propeller plane pulled an advertisement for a local classical concert series. The sky was clear, blue, majestic. There was no lifeguard but a sign that said to swim at your own risk. Many did. We walked a half-mile up the beach to the Dune Deck, as I would with Celia, and drank vodka martinis and listened to the European children staying in the old hotel beg their parents for more ice cream. Back at home, we had sex on the dining table. Afterward, Leah prepared a caprese with the most beautiful tomatoes; I panfried a halibut. For dessert, there was peach cobbler. We drank wine now, staring out at the ocean, in silence.

"How are you doing?" asked Leah.

"I'm happy to be here."

"Good. So am I."

"Good."

"*Good.*"

After lunch, Leah and I bicycled into town. There was an old diner near the movie theater, and we drank coffee at the counter, just as Celia and I had often done on rainy days. We rode back home past fishermen who stood on the bridge with their lines lowered into the bay. Leah wore a white cotton dress, and I took it off her the moment we got inside. We had sex on the floor. Then we brought out cheese and bread, figs and melon, and drank more wine and stared out at the beach and the ocean. Celia used to paint on this very porch while I read beside her. Those were some of the best days. Today, a large canvas Celia had ordered would be delivered. She was making a full-sized portrait of Dom.

At some point Leah went inside to make a phone call. Listening to her, I was reminded of the calls Celia would make to Graham. Away two days, it would have been time to check in. That was one of their rules, as it was now one of ours. Because Celia and I had a child to consider, our rules were slightly different than the ones she'd had with Graham: You had to be home for dinner, and you couldn't go out before Waylon was asleep. You had to always be home by morning: when Waylon woke up, he should find both his parents in bed. Say, for instance, Celia was out at night and Waylon was asleep in his bed, I couldn't have Leah over. How could I be away with Leah now? Graham and Celia had flown down to Athens, Georgia, for a college reunion, and they had taken Waylon along with them. I could have gone, too. Celia had asked me to come, and I wondered now if Dom had made the trip in my stead.

    Celia had told me about her life with Graham back at the University of Georgia, how their relationship was started on long walks in the Georgia woods, lake-swims, conversations on art. Their second summer together they were invited to Italy by a professor, a filmmaker who offered to pay their airfare and lodging if they acted in his production. They flew to Tuscany. Celia had never been outside the country before, and she felt that life was finally happening for her. The town was paved in cobblestone and surrounded by crenelated walls at the top of a very steep hill. Cypresses grew tall on the periphery. The movie was shot in the daytime and the director, an old, hypochondriacal man, worked them hard under the big hot sun. But at night they ate twelve course meals, and on their first week off Celia and Graham went by bus to Rome. They hurried through the city, trying to see it all. They took a boat to Sardinia. They didn't have much money, and the boatman let them ride for free. They ate tuna from a can, which Graham opened with his pocketknife. They slept on the beach and when they woke, a wild boar was passing right by their sandy heads. The sea was calm, and they swam to get clean. A local shopkeeper took pity and gave them coffee and doughnuts for breakfast. They hadn't even asked for anything; they were young and in love and looked like they were in need, was how Celia had described it. A bus that came only three times a week brought them back to the small Tuscan village. How happy they were to return there. They went to the restaurant in town. Out of money, Celia and Graham were told they could pay another time. It was on their way home that night that Graham proposed to Celia. He said that yes, they were young, but that he was certain that he wanted to spend his whole life with her. So then why wait? He reached into his pocket and took out a plain white band which he'd bought just one week earlier while in Rome. Celia extended her ring finger and let him slide on the band. The wedding was not the small ceremony they had first discussed, there were two hundred people. Celia's grandfather, a minister, who had walked with Martin Luther King, Jr. from Selma, married them in the backyard behind the Victorian mansion in which they lived on the outskirts of Athens, Georgia, a home said to be haunted by dead soldiers of the Civil War. Celia fought with her mother. The party went until morning. With classes due to start back up, they skipped a honeymoon. To already have a husband and be only a junior in college was greatly satisfying to Celia; she considered herself to be ahead of her peers. But after college, she and Graham moved to New York City, and suddenly Celia felt too young to be married. She wanted to see other men, to explore. When she told Graham, he didn't know what she could possibly mean. He was slow to realize his own feelings. Celia was already seeing someone (this was a year before she and I began to date after meeting at a Christmas party). She asked Graham if he would like to see other women. *Other women?* What would Graham want with them? Graham had one woman, the greatest woman, and he had no interest in any other. And though he agreed to the new arrangement, one year later he still had not slept with another woman. Now, having sex with Leah in the kitchen, I finally understood why Graham had remained monogamous in his open marriage.

That afternoon the beach became so dense with fog we couldn't see, and we might have thought we were in the clouds. Our feet were gone. If we raised our hands overhead they vanished from sight. Leah and I walked back to the Dune Deck. The sand squeaked under our feet, and I felt the moisture on my face. The Dune Deck was three jetties down-beach. A lifeguard chair stood wet and forlorn among rows of unoccupied beach furniture. Leah and I sat at a table on the deck, the only people here. Despite the weather, the waiter didn't seem surprised to see us. Our order: two vodka martinis, grilled octopus, French fries. We began to talk about our eating since arriving here, our drinking, too. Was it excessive? We were indulging. After we finished, around six o'clock, we took a taxi into town and bowled. I had seen Celia throw many gutters on these lanes, all of them charming. Leah and I drank beer, and the machine kept score. We had sex out back behind the bowling alley between two parked cars, then went home.

The following morning was muggy, hot. Breakfast was fresh berries and strong coffee. Seated on the deck, staring out at the ocean, Leah told me how her father used to take her sailing. It was difficult to focus on her story. One time Celia and I had been sitting right here having a breakfast much like the one Leah and I were having now, and she told me about how Graham didn't want to claim her and I said that to claim a person could make them feel valued and loved.

"Are you listening to me?" said Leah.

"I am."

"Then what did I just say, Paul? You don't know, do you? Where are you right now? All weekend, it's felt like you've been someplace else."

"I'm sorry," I said. "I promise, I'm here. Say it again. I swear to you, I won't miss another word."

21
To Have It All

Celia and I became pariahs almost immediately, a couple to be kept away from at all costs. To be in our company was to be swept up into the conversation of whether monogamy was possible or even natural. Our mere presence would send couples home fighting. Or so our friends would tell me, usually in fits of rage. They could no longer spend time with us *as* couples. It was too dangerous. Celia and I had become symbols of all the most threatening questions. Such as: Which of our married friends still had sex? And who felt any desire at all for their spouses? And who didn't want to trade her life to have sex with someone other than her spouse for even just a night? In one-on-one situations, though, with friends and non-friends, I would be questioned vigorously. How had I pulled this off? To keep my family *and* get to sleep around?

I took no credit. Celia had been the one to suggest that we open our relationship. I had only agreed to it because I hadn't seen another way forward for us. Sure, I was sleeping with Leah, and we had gone away together. Also, three or four times-a-week, she and I would meet at her apartment, sometimes in the morning, sometimes the afternoon or evening, to have sex. And where the experience had had its momentary thrills, I couldn't report back to anyone that this newfound sexual freedom had benefited my life.

"I don't believe you, Paul. I don't fucking believe you don't love every minute of it."

My employer, the real estate activist, Cal Lowenstein, hosted a regular get-together for friends and colleagues. Partners and children were invited, and Celia and Waylon had come along with me on this Saturday afternoon. I hadn't seen either of them in over twenty minutes. Perhaps they were out back in the yard or on one of the other floors of the Beekman Place townhouse. Lowenstein's wife, Wanda, was a successful plastic surgeon. She and Celia got along just fine. They could have even been having the same conversation as me and Lowenstein. What a disturbing thought.

"I wonder where my family is," I said.

"They're here somewhere. Don't worry about them. I finally have you to myself. And you know my wife and I no longer have sex. You *know* that."

Lowenstein, a snarling, compact man, below average height, short dark hair, a full beard, liked to tell me about how he and his wife no longer had sex. He would then list off the things that he *did* have.

"We're selling the house in Nantucket and getting the new one in East Hampton, Paul."

"Uh-huh."

"And I just got my season tickets for the Knicks for next year."

"That's great."

"But my wife won't touch me, so what's any of it worth?"

"I'm sorry, Cal. I'd say if you love your wife—or even just like her—figure out a way to stay together."

"I was afraid you'd say that."

A few months back, Lowenstein had told me that he'd been thinking about asking out a woman. It was then that I had mistakenly let him in on my own situation and explained how Celia and I had opened our relationship and how ultimately the arrangement had been doing severe and irreversible damage to my life ever since. And now he had me at the back of his kitchen, a long, narrow slot, and was blocking my return to the party. Panting, enraged, he said, "I'm not going to do it, Paul. I'm not going to ask this woman out. At least not before I talk to Wanda about it."

"Well, I don't recommend that either."

"But why not?" he shouted. "We could *both* be fucking."

"Because it doesn't work, Cal. It's too painful, honestly. You and your wife will just end up hurting each other. If you still care at all about this person—if you care *at all*, which I'm sure you *both* do—then these actions are going to cause pain. You can either choose to ignore that pain or you can confront it. But either way, it's going to be there, burning a hole through your life."

"There's already a hole being burnt through my life, Paul. What's another hole?"

I shook my head. "I'm telling you, Cal. Take my word for it or don't, but—"

"Maybe it's just that it doesn't work for you and Celia."

"Maybe so. Maybe it would work for you and Wanda. But just do me a favor, Cal, whatever you do, if you bring this up with Wanda, leave me out of it, please."

Lowenstein chuckled. He said, "I wouldn't have to mention you by name. Everyone knows about you and Celia. We're all talking about it, Paul, and we're all thinking about it. I practically invited you both here today so that I could have the conversation with Wanda after you left. Don't be upset with me. I'm just a human being. I just want to be loved, Paul. I just want to be loved."

22

The Rules

"No, sleepovers. That's the rule, Celia. That's the *most* important rule."

She couldn't hear me now. I was speaking to myself, alone in bed, staring at the digital clock on the nightstand: 3:16 in the morning. In one minute, it would be 3:17, and a minute later, 3:18. I could not stop looking at the clock. Where was Celia? Was she okay? Was she alive? Surely, she was. But then I wouldn't be at ease until she was here with me.

"Come on, where are you?" I said, aloud.

I had fallen asleep around midnight but woke thirty minutes ago, heart pounding, back sweaty, mind churning. My eyes had been locked on the digital red numbers since. I had texted her twice. No reply. I texted again.

Did Celia lay awake at night like this waiting for me to return? She had told me recently that, yes, she couldn't settle in either until I was in bed next to her. Since opening our relationship, though, I was positive that I had waited up many more nights than she had.

"3:19…3:20…3:21…"

The following morning, a Sunday, still in bed, I was awoken by the feeling of Celia drawing herself close to me. I hadn't heard her come in last night. I must have fallen asleep while watching the clock. For the first time in what felt like years, Celia began saying how we really should get married.

"You actually think so?"

"I do, Paul."

"You came in the door three hours ago after being out all night with Dom, and now you're talking about us getting married?"

"That's right."

Roughly a week ago, Celia had told me she couldn't imagine herself *not* being with a woman. What about that? Did she envision us spending the rest of our lives having so many relationships at once?

"No," said Celia. "I don't know. Just marry me, please. I want to get married."

"I don't see why we should get married, not if you *have* to be with women."

"*Shh*. Just please, let's get married. I want to get married."

"Did you get into some terrible argument with Dom? Is that what this is about?"

"No," said Celia.

Dom and Celia had been fighting a lot these days. Dom was not doing well with the current arrangement, hadn't come all this way from Poland to be the woman on the side. She wanted more. How much more? The whole thing. For Celia to leave me and to be with her and only her. She often challenged Celia. *Celia*, she said, was gay. Who was she kidding? And to be walking around in the world, parading herself about as someone involved with a man, with her *perfect* family, was obscene and disgusting. About a month ago, Celia had begun to see a therapist so that she could investigate her sexuality and find out about the life she wanted for herself. She admitted to feeling tremendous pressure to figure it all out quickly.

"And do you and your therapist talk about us getting married?"

"Paul."

"It's an honest question."

"No, we don't," she said. "But *I* think we should get married. Will you marry me?"

At which point I said *fine* and Celia thanked me, and then we made love and finished just seconds before our son came barreling into the room. We happily greeted Waylon, squeezing the child in our arms. Celia then suggested that we put a lock on our bedroom door. I agreed that it probably *was* time for a lock.

And so after our morning together, I went off to the hardware store. Walking along industrial streets, I thought about marrying Celia and the preposterousness of her suggestion. What was *all that* about? Then it dawned on me: I was about to lose her, wasn't I? My family and home, too. Soon it would be just me—me and my cursed corners—and nothing else. Well, I did love my cursed corners. And yes, alone with my cursed corners, I would make my newsletter even better. I would like to see its reach expand so that soon I was covering cursed corners in other cities in the United

States. Every city had its cursed corners. I could head out on the road, visit every part of the country, identify those corners and write about them in my newsletter.

No. In a book.

I would make a book. A *big* book. One where I would document every cursed corner in the United States. That was it. That was *something*. And hardly nothing. It was a great big project. This was the beauty of work, it was always there for you no matter what you lost. It was a safety net constructed over years through diligence and perseverance, and it would catch you at your worst times, suspend you in mid-air and then put you back on solid ground.

But was there any better place than the hardware store? They had everything in these aisles, ladders and saws and ceiling fans, but also plants and outdoor patio furniture. The knowledgeable employees could instruct you on how to put in a new toilet or how to prepare your pipes for a long winter. Meanwhile, you could have some lumber cut to size and a set of keys made while you waited. And what a selection of locks—there were so many to choose from. But then to do so was especially difficult now, for I was fantasizing about cursed corners in Chicago and Los Angeles, San Francisco, Portland, and Austin. And what about those in Atlanta? Miami? Nashville? Washington, DC? Boston? Wouldn't a publisher just jump at the opportunity to put out this book? Besides, my newsletter already had a loyal fan base in New York. Why shouldn't a book like this sell? Oh, I couldn't wait to begin this project. I had to get out there and hunt. After all, humans were natural hunters, and not just for bedroom door locks.

Having found the one I needed, I brought it up to the cashier to pay. Taking a credit card from my wallet, my hands shook. I was so excited about this book on cursed corners that I could hardly contain myself. I had discovered my grand new purpose in life. The idea had fallen out of the sky, and I had been there, hands out, ready to receive it.

Yes, I had been saved.

23
Threats

You think you're so clever, don't you.
You messed with the wrong person.
This isn't going to end well for you, Paul.
I wouldn't walk the streets alone.
I wouldn't walk the streets at all.
I'd leave New York City and go into hiding.
That's what I'd do if I were you.
That's the best shot you have at living.
There's no getting away with what you've done.
No Getting Away With It.
So, who's cursed now?
You're cursed.
You!
Write one more cursed corner,
And you're dead.
I mean it.

"Paul, I'm sorry. I'm really very sorry. We're doing the best we can with the situation. Hang in there." It was Cal Lowenstein on the phone. A letter threatening my life had been received at his office. "We always knew there was a danger to what you were doing. You're messing with people's money, their billion-dollar investments. But don't worry because the FBI is already looking through all the buildings you've profiled, and we'll see what they come up with."

I had just dropped Waylon at kindergarten and was standing outside the red brick schoolhouse amid a crowd of screaming children. Though I knew Lowenstein to have a hands-behind-the-head, feet-up-on-the-desk kind of arrogance, I hoped, in the case of this call, the man had the decency to be stooped in his office chair. Regardless, I didn't care about the letter, and I told Lowenstein as much.

"Of course, you don't care, Paul. You're out there having as much sex as you like. *You're* in charge."

"That's not what I meant at all."

"Well, you won't mind then if we put the newsletter on hiatus."

"On *hiatus!*" Had I heard Lowenstein correctly? Children were swarming my legs and falling over each other and shouting.

"Paul, don't worry. You just go out there and get laid as much as you can and forget the newsletter for six months. It'll fly by. I mean, you have to understand that if I let you continue to write the newsletter and you get hurt or God forbid murdered by this person making these threats against your life, your family and I will have a serious problem."

"Oh, Cal, please, don't do this. I was just about to start writing a whole book on cursed corners. I was going to hit the road and document all the cursed corners in the country."

"No, no, no, no, no, Paul. *That* can't happen. No more cursed corners for now. No more posts about cursed corners on social media. You will go silent until given further notice. Got it? Now go out there and have sex with a beautiful stranger. That's just what'll get you through all of this. God, I envy you, Paul. You have got it good, my friend. You have got it good."

I didn't quite take Lowenstein's advice, but I did call up Leah—and I was now reciting the letter aloud to her, the two of us lying naked in her bed at one-thirty on a Wednesday afternoon.

"Paul, this is terrible." Leah threw off the bed covers, her pulsing blue watery eyes staring back at me with concern.

"It's strange, isn't it?"

"It's worse than *strange*."

"Maybe a little alarming."

"No, no—it is *very* alarming."

Thankfully, I had Leah's support now. She was someone who could buffer me from the added stress of these new and unusual circumstances. Her bedroom was a comfort to me, too: the small glass chandelier hanging above the bed, the dried flowers in the vase on the mantle, the purple yoga blocks stacked in the corner, the smell of her perfume in the sheets. I was just so grateful to have Leah to talk to about the death threats; Celia hadn't seemed too concerned. Perhaps she was too busy, too in love, to care. She had never been so interested in cursed corners, anyway. But to have Leah in my life, this good friend, was so valuable to me now.

"But no, Paul, I'm *not* your friend," said Leah. "We're lovers. That means we have sex and that's it, nothing more.

And now who knows what you may have gotten me mixed up in. Did you check and see if anyone was trailing you on your way over here?"

"Trailing me? *Who* would trail me?"

"The person making threats against your life, Paul. Someone might have seen you come into my apartment. You're not taking this seriously enough. You have to start."

"Okay, I will." But in all likelihood, someone was just having a little fun with me. Why write a menacing letter? Who was I really? The author of a newsletter? This was a stunt. A gimmick, a ploy. And it was working. I had lost my newsletter, hadn't I? And maybe my lover, too?

"I don't know. *Yes*, you probably have," said Leah. She enjoyed having sex with me but made clear she was not going to risk her life for it. That made sense to me, didn't it? "You understand, don't you?"

"I guess so. I mean, sure, yes, I do."

She kissed me on the forehead, then gave me a light shove out of the bed. She said that if I got the situation straightened out that I could call her. "But I have a mother and father, and they can't lose their daughter because of some fling like the one we've been having."

"Fling?"

"Yes, Paul. You understand, don't you?"

"Yes, right, *a fling*," I said. "I understand."

"Thank you, Paul. I knew you would." Her eyes softened, her brow settled, her jaw released some tension, and she smiled at me. "I'm going to take a shower. You can let yourself out."

24

Under Water

A friendly reminder that,
Writing cursed corners,
Will get you killed,
Paul.

The downstairs front door buzzer was ringing. It was the kind of aggressive, impatient ring that caused the blood pressure to rise. I wasn't expecting anyone. Perhaps it was a package. Waylon was in the bath and Celia was in her studio at the back working on a painting for the group show at the Chelsea gallery next month. She was occupied, in the middle of something, with several brushes in her left hand all with paint on them, doing a highly detailed part of Dom's lips. She wouldn't know to save her son should he begin to drown. That was my duty, the explanation for why I was standing at the bathroom door and looking in on the child every few seconds in between chopping up cilantro and onion for taco night.

Again, the buzzer.

I startled. Celia yelled out from the back. Was I going to get the door or what!

No, I would not get the door. For one thing, because our son was in the bath and for another, in addition to the cilantro and the onion, there were limes and avocados to slice and meat to season and cook. Furthermore, there could be someone downstairs who intended to bash in my skull. Two days ago, a second threatening letter had arrived at Lowenstein's office. At the market a few hours earlier, I could have sworn someone was following me. And perhaps this ringing buzzer confirmed it. I set the knife in my right hand down on the kitchen counter to stop it from shaking.

The buzzer sounded a third time.

Celia cried out once again for me to get the door. But I shouted back at her that I couldn't get the door because Waylon was in the bath *and* there was meat cooking in a pan. And though the meat was not yet cooking, I switched on the flame and began heating up the pan. Then I went to look at our child and was horrified to see him under the water in the tub.

"What the hell are you doing, Waylon?" I grabbed him into an upright position.

"Dad, why'd you do that! I was trying to see how long I could hold my breath."

"Well, stop! Not now. We'll do it together another time."

"I want to break my record."

"*No!* Now don't mess around."

Had I just heard the front door at the bottom of the stairs swing open? And was that the sound of two people speaking to each other? Had a neighbor, some lamb-like new resident of New York City, done the asinine thing and allowed a stranger to walk inside the building and given access to my would-be assailant? The stairs beyond the apartment door creaked. I grabbed the knife off the counter, slid it into my pocket, tip down. I walked to the door and opened it a crack. Someone was coming toward the apartment. I slammed the door. And now someone was knocking.

Bang. Bang. Bang.

"Hello," I said. "Who's there? Who's there! What do you want?"

Suddenly, a large flame shot up the edge of the pan. I sprang back into the kitchen and shut the gas and pushed the pan to a back burner, scalding myself. Checking the bathroom, I saw that Waylon was under the water again. I shouted at him that he better listen to me or else.

Bang. Bang. Bang.

"Who are you?"

Bang. Bang. Bang.

"Why are you here!"

"Paul," said the voice. It was a woman. "Paul, open the door right now."

Did I know this person? Not by the sound of her voice alone. But I was no longer afraid. I took a deep breath and opening the door I was at once smacked in the face.

"Ow, *fuck*."

"You goddamn lowlife. You sonofabitch!"

It was Wanda Lowenstein. She wore a gray sweatsuit with the hood drawn tightly around her head, her eyebrows thick and dark. She was standing eye to eye with me and screaming, "What did you tell my husband? What crazy idea did you put into his head!"

I allowed Wanda to jab me repeatedly in the chest with a forefinger while I promised I hadn't told Cal a thing.

"Bullshit. You're lying. You're lying to me."

"Why don't you come in and sit down?"

"I don't want to come in and sit down! You're a bastard. I know what you did. You told my husband how fucking wonderful it is that you and your wife can go around fucking whoever you want whenever you want—"

"Hey, hey, hey, I didn't tell him anything like that," I said. Now *I* was pointing my finger at Wanda. This would only rile her up more, and so I slid both hands into my pockets. It took no time at all to register the sharp blade slicing open my right hand. The knife—I had forgotten that it was in that pocket. There wasn't any pain yet, but the blood was already gushing, and Wanda was shouting louder and louder at me about the rupture I had caused to her marriage.

"I have to check on my son, Wanda. I'm sorry, please, just hold on."

I left Wanda at the door and poked my head into the bathroom to find Waylon still under the water.

"Waylon! What the hell!"

He slid up out of the water, hair matted to his face. He was smiling. "Dad, I broke my record!"

"Good job. I'm really proud of you. But please, *enough!*"

I could feel my hand throbbing. I wouldn't look at the wound, I didn't want to know its severity. I grabbed a towel and tied it around my hand.

"Dad, your hand is bleeding."

"I know, I know, I know."

I took another glance at my son and then a deep breath, girding myself for more of Wanda's furious accusations; however, now Celia was shouting at Wanda, defending my character, my honor, my life.

"Yes, but, Celia, *I* know how men talk to each other," Wanda was saying, "and it's all 'I fucked her like that' and 'Oh, I stuck it in her in like this.' That's the cancer your husband put in my husband's head."

"That does *not* sound like Paul, not even a little," said Celia. "Anyway, after we left your home the last time, Paul complained to me about how Cal was after him the whole party, cornering him to talk about *our* relationship and how it worked because he was intent on talking to you about changing your arrangement. Paul found it all very disturbing."

"You're lying."

"I'm not," said Celia. "And besides, you've been with Cal a long time. You're really going to come here tonight and blame your marital issues on Paul? Get a grip. Paul doesn't know you, and I doubt he even likes your husband."

"You're a bitch."

The door slammed. I emerged from the bathroom and took a good long look at Celia, clapping my hands and declaring her beauty. Celia's expression was one of exasperation, but also humor, relief. That was until she noticed my wound. The towel had fallen off my hand and blood was running from my palm down my forearm to the elbow. I told Celia not to worry, I couldn't feel a thing, there was no pain whatsoever. I was just so proud of her. She had handled the situation calmly while striking at will. I leaned in to kiss her, but she took me firmly by the wrist, inspecting the gash on my hand.

"Paul," she cried, "we have to get you to the hospital!"

25

Who Have I Become

Eight stitches. Not so bad.

The doctor had instructed me to avoid using my right hand until the wound had had a chance to heal. Two weeks, maybe longer. To be down to just my left hand would be difficult under any circumstances, but now I was taking care of Waylon without the help of Celia for the weekend. And where was she? In Detroit, staying in the house where Dom had lived the first eighteen years of her life. Dom had been looking forward to introducing her to her parents and friends for months, and she would never let Celia postpone just because I had hurt my hand. If Celia had mentioned the possibility of it, Dom would have flipped out. Dom had never brought a girlfriend home to stay for the weekend. Her parents could hardly acknowledge that their daughter was gay. Dom had been preparing her heart for this and was ready to take the leap—with Celia, who had promised to help her every step of the way.

But then who would help me with the jar of peanut butter I was trying to open right now? I could hear Waylon calling out to me from his bedroom. The child was hungry for lunch.

It wasn't five minutes later, though, that Graham showed up at the apartment. What was he doing here? It seemed that Celia had called him earlier in the morning and told him I could probably use him around the house today.

"She was absolutely wrong. I'm fine, Graham. I don't need your help. You have to leave right now."

"Paul, please, let me help you. You look like you're under a lot of stress."

Graham should have been worried about himself. He looked bad, scraggly beard, gaunt, long brown hair knotted, shoes coming apart. But his focus was on me and me alone. Maybe I seemed worse than him. He said, "Paul, I'd like to help you. It looks to me like you could really use some help."

Graham was walking toward me, reaching for the same jar of peanut butter.

"Stay back!" I shouted. "Stay away from me, Graham. Don't get any closer."

"Paul, what's going on with you? Let me help you."

"No, Graham. Please, no, no, no, no. Oh, Graham! Graham." I slumped down over the dining table, banging my fists. "Don't you see, Graham! Don't you get it? I...I...I've turned into you. I've fucking turned into *you*."

"I don't understand. What do you mean?"

"What do you *mean* what do I mean? Isn't it obvious!"

The pain in my left hand shot up into my shoulder then. I let out a cry.

Waylon bounded joyfully into the kitchen now and jumped right up into Graham's arms. "Hi, Graham."

"Hi, Waylon. How are you, my good friend?"

"I'm great. Happy to see you."

"I'm happy to see you, too."

I stared at them both and then, with my head lowered, stuck the closed jar of peanut butter into Graham's chest. "I have to take a nap. You two have lunch."

—

I woke an hour later, warm, disoriented, and in pain. Graham and Waylon were making watercolors in the kitchen. I didn't have the strength to even say hello but stood in the doorway, listening.

"She'll be coming home soon," Graham was saying. "And let me tell you, if she were stranded anywhere—and I mean anywhere—even the North Pole, I would go and find her and bring her back to you."

"You would?" said Waylon.

"I sure would. And if she were stuck on the moon, I would talk to NASA about how a guy like me gets use of a rocket ship and I would take that rocket ship and fly it to the moon and bring your mom home."

"You can't have a rocket ship."

"Who says? I need one. It's an emergency. And if your mom were lost in the Sahara Desert, I would lead a search team, a great big search team, and we would find her and bring her back home to you."

"You really would?"

"Of course I would."

"And how far away is she?"

"Well, not so far. Not so far at all. Now that's a great watercolor you've got going. What is that? An ocean with licorice sticks swimming it?"

"No. It's a sky with flying birds."

"I think it's just great, my friend."

"You do?"

"I sure do."

At the next moment, I slipped away and went back to bed.

—

Sometime later—the sound of the apartment's front door slamming shut—and I shot upright in the bed. The room was dark. I couldn't see out into the kitchen. Who was here? Was it the man who meant to kill me? I heard a woman.

Nicole, Graham's girlfriend.

She was screaming: that Celia would be off in another state and I would be asleep in bed while Graham babysat our child, it was despicable. Didn't Graham get it? Celia and I were vultures, willing to feed on him forever and ever. Nicole begged him to see the truth. She was trying to save him. He didn't have to remain under our spell any longer. She was offering him a way out of this awful cycle of abuse that had begun years ago.

"Nicole, please, don't talk like this to me. I can't take it when you get this way. None of that's true. Waylon is the son of my very good friend. Of course I want a relationship with him. Of course I want to care for him. We're *family*."

"Goddamn it, Graham, *stop it* already. You're so fucking blind. Anyone can see it. I mean *anyone*. You treat him like the son you wished you'd had with Celia. You think of him as yours—as yours and Celia's."

"No, no, no, you don't get it—"

"I get it. I get it all. Now please stop, Graham. Just stop. You and me, we can leave New York and go down South and get you far away from these people who suck your life-force and leave you dried up and empty."

"Nicole, no, I can't leave right now. I'm here with Waylon."

"Where even is that child of yours?"

"Don't call him that. I can't stand when you call him that. Waylon's in bed. I was just about to read him a story. There are so many books we like to read together, Nicole. It's one of our special things. I love reading to that child."

"Oh, Graham. Graham, Graham, Graham. *Okay*, do what you have to do—read the kid a book. But as soon as you can, just come home to me. Come to me, okay, Graham? Promise you'll come right away. Then I want to begin discussing how we're going to leave New York."

"Okay, Nicole. Okay. I will come to you. I promise."

"And we can begin that discussion?"

"Yes. If that's what you'd like."

"Thank you. I would like that. I love you so much, Graham."

"I love you, too, Nicole."

After another minute I heard the front door close. Pretending to sleep, that I hadn't heard a thing, was the least I could do for Graham.

But then I couldn't help myself.

"Graham," I called out to him, "that woman is going to save your life. You better go with her. You better go with her right now. Get out of here. *Go!*"

26
Couples Therapy

Celia had been in therapy for about four months. She believed the benefits had been substantial. She found her sessions inspired and healing. She went twice a week and would arrive home after in a positively chipper mood. She was closer to determining who she was and what she needed out of life.

"Who am I? What do I want? How will I get it? I'll know soon enough."

This was what she said to me, not once, but following almost every session. And I was happy for her, proud to see Celia making these kinds of difficult strides. She was figuring out her past, present, and future. She was discovering her sense of how she should be, piecing together a methodology, a philosophy, sorting through her pain, her joy, motherhood, career, relationships, friendships, ex-husbands, partners, lovers, *everything*. I lived on the sideline of her psychological journey, clapping along encouragingly. This was real growth. I loved every minute of it, largely because I believed it would help our relationship and convince her that what she needed above all else moving forward was our home, our life, *us*.

One day, Celia came in the door following a therapy session and said she needed me to come with her the next time and would I be open to it. Her tone was serious, almost stern. Her face revealed some plot, her eyes glaring, the tip of her tongue pressed against her top teeth, perhaps to let out some tension, some fear. My heart began to race.

"We have to have a very important talk. I think it would be best if it happened there."

"Are you sure this is a good idea?"

"I think it's a very good idea," said Celia.

She had cut off about two feet of hair the previous week and now had a chin-length do. The change was dramatic. I almost couldn't recognize her. Leaning against the kitchen counter, she kept touching the ends, nervously. I brought my hands through my own thick, tangled hair now, sighing.

"Will I like your therapist?"

"Paul, she's wonderful. You'll get along well, I'm sure."

"Will it conflict with my schedule?"

"What schedule? You have no schedule."

"Okay—but who will watch Waylon? We need to give Graham a break. He's been taking too many babysitting shifts."

"We'll hire a sitter," said Celia. "I'll take care of that."

I thought for another moment but couldn't come up with any other excuses.

Three days later, the time came. Celia's therapist, Molly, worked out of a small studio in the neighborhood with a view of the East River and the Williamsburg Bridge. She wasn't much older than we were. Brown bob, blue eyes, her pastel-colored dress hung loosely on her body. She greeted us with a nod of the head. Almost immediately after being invited to sit down and make ourselves comfortable, Celia began to weep. She held my hand tightly. After taking a moment to blow her nose, to wipe her tears, to breathe deeply, Celia looked at Molly and spoke about her struggles to figure out whether she was gay, straight, bi, in love with Dom, or in love with me and our family, or in love with *all* of us. She was desperate to get free from all this uncertainty, she said, then collapsed onto my shoulder, crying hard.

And now I was sobbing, too. I could see how much pain Celia was in. Did she need me to set her free? Was that it? To hear me say that she must go off and be *herself*, whoever that was? I couldn't bear the thought of losing her. I couldn't stand the idea that our family should break up. I knew how much pain that thought brought to her as well. But I wouldn't let her think for a moment that I was all right with such an outcome. And I said so now, as the two of us continued to weep and hold one another.

"I love him so much. I love our family. I just don't know what to do. I don't know. It's killing me," Celia told Molly.

The therapist asked Celia to turn to me and tell *me*. And so Celia did just that—and we cried, holding one another for a long time.

But then Celia wasn't done speaking. Something very important had been on her mind for a while and was causing her a lot of stress, and she had to say it now: the group show at the Chelsea gallery was next week. Dom was her girlfriend and Celia loved her. Dom was also in all four paintings included in the show. Celia could not exclude Dom from such an important night.

"She has to be there," said Celia.

"Well, you can invite her," I said, "but then *I* won't be there."

This wasn't the answer Celia was looking for. "Please, you have to be there, Paul. This is such a big moment for me. I've been working so hard to get to this place. You know that. This is over ten years of struggling, all that hard work coming to fruition."

"I know that."

"You wouldn't miss it then."

"I'm not going to stand in that room with you and Dom, Celia. You have to choose: either me and our family, or Dom."

"Come on, Paul. Just think about it, please."

"No. I don't have to. I've got my mind made up."

Celia tried again later that evening and again while we drank coffee in bed the following morning. I reiterated that I would not be at the opening if Dom were attending, too. Celia insisted Dom would be there and if that was too much for me, then she understood, and I didn't have to come, but I should also know that my absence would ruin her night. I *had* to know that, too. There were tears in her eyes. It was now that she chose to inform me that the gallery had offered her a solo exhibition next year. It was confirmed, yes: a solo show at a very good Chelsea gallery in the prime month of September. Her painting career was finally taking off. This night would mark the start of that ascent.

"Please, be there. Celebrate this moment with me."

"No, I can't do it. I just can't. It won't be a celebration, not for me."

"But you would be doing it for me."

"In front of all our friends, our family. No, it's impossible, Celia. I don't want them to see us like this."

"But they have to grow, too. They have to see that we've changed, that we're not the same people nor the same couple. It's okay for them to see that change, to understand who we are now."

"No, it's not. Not for me. Not like that. Not on your big night. That doesn't work for me, Celia," I said. "If you invite Dom, I won't be there. That's it."

The Brill Building

Curse, I want you to know that it's always been a labor of love. Since day one, I've enjoyed every minute of it. I would have done it for free. But I'm also getting very antsy. I feel like I might have to do something inadvisable—the kind of thing that could set off a murderer—and disseminate my findings to my mailing list. You would understand, wouldn't you? You wouldn't turn your back on me if I did, right? We're in this together forever, aren't we, Curse? Because what about The Brill Building? Right, Curse? What about it!

Once the very epicenter of the music industry, it was inside this Deco wonder where some of the greatest songwriters to ever grace the planet once crammed into tiny offices to write the biggest hits of all-time. "Yakety Yak" was penned here. "Breaking Up Is Hard to Do!" "The Loco-Motion!" Burt Bacharach and Carole King and Marvin Hamlisch and Neil Diamond and Bobby Darin, The Ronettes, The Shirelles, The Shangri-Las, Dionne Warwick, Frankie Valli and the Four Seasons—you could bump into any one of these legends in the halls of this holy site. What were they doing there? Writing or recording hits, naturally.

The Brill Building was a bona fide hit-factory and only those with the goods were granted entry. Following the boom years of the 1950s and 1960s, the songwriters, recording studios, record labels, and publishing companies slowly began to vanish. The times were a-changing, and the industry was, too, and the Brill Building began to grow quiet. After so many fallow years, the bell finally tolled with the closing of Colony

Records, the iconic record store on the building's ground floor corner location. And what's come up in the place of Colony? A two-story CVS? Oh, Curse, is it over? Is it all really over? Won't you save us just one last dance?

27

A Savior

I'll never understand why,
You couldn't have listened to me,
Paul.
You must be trying,
To end your life.

Celia put a lot of time and effort over the next few days into finishing the four paintings for the group show. She also sent out invitations, bought a new dress, and booked a hair and nail appointment for the day of. She made no requests of me. She was keeping me at a distance. A respectful distance? Respectful or not, it didn't especially matter—she was, simply put, no longer including me in her life. She would come into the apartment and busy herself with her work—or with calls, emails, the recycling of old mail—and not say hello to me. She was taking her meals in the studio, breezing into the kitchen for more salt, more pepper, a fresh napkin, and disappearing again without acknowledging my presence. And then in bed, in the evening, she lay with her back to me—no more holding each other, no more talking or laughing or saying *goodnight*. All that was out.

Celia wasn't the only person slipping away from me. Lowenstein was furious about my recent newsletter on the Brill Building. He called my actions indefensible, dangerous. He was *firing* me. Or, as he put it, "giving me the axe." He took the opportunity over the phone to say how unhappy he'd been with my work of late: the writing, he said, had become overly personalized, increasingly bitter, and yet somehow more sentimental, too. He didn't offer one positive word about the work I had done for him throughout all the years, didn't assure me of a recommendation for a next employer, said nothing about wishing me good luck in my future endeavors to come, didn't ask me if I had any prospects or any money to pay my bills this month. He didn't even tell me to go out there and have sex with a beautiful woman. He just hung up.

As for the new death threat, I hadn't told Celia. She was not the person to talk to now about this or anything. And who could I turn to for help? If not Celia, nor Leah, nor Cal Lowenstein, nor my mother—then who? *Who* could save me now?

Confronted with this question and with night falling over Manhattan, I went to ring the doorbell of Leah's benefactor, Rick Miller. During Leah's book party, Miller had put me on notice, no? Telling me that he had a personal relationship with the owners of the very buildings I had "cursed" and that I had to be careful about antagonizing them because they were dangerous people—hadn't he warned me about everything to come? He had, yes. But then he might know the letter writer, too. Maybe it was Miller himself doing it. In which case I would happily beg for his forgiveness.

Miller's townhouse looked even better when he wasn't hosting a party. Without the swing music and all the guests milling about, his home was quiet and still. I didn't have an appointment, but I had already been led inside by a tall, gray-haired man in a black suit who asked me to wait in the foyer. That had been about ten minutes ago.

"Hello," I called out. "Is anyone up there?"

At last, the gray-haired man appeared. He was three flights up and leaning over the banister. He apologized for the wait, and for Miller, who would not be able to see me this evening. "He is otherwise disposed."

"Can you tell me a good time to come back?"

"Mr. Miller doesn't keep normal hours. His schedule fluctuates. Would you like to leave a message with a number where you can be reached?"

"Can you give me pen and paper? I'll write it down for you."

"Just call the numbers up," said the gray-haired man. "I'll remember."

"You'll remember my phone number? Oh, okay. Sure." Saying the first of the numbers, trying to loft them up to where the gray-haired man stood, I felt foolish and a little bit defeated. But I continued through all the digits. "Do you want to repeat the number back to me?"

"No, no, I assure you I've got it. But Mr. Miller will want to know the purpose of your visit this evening so that he can better address your needs. Would you like to give me a brief summation that I can relay to him?"

"That would be great," I said, beginning to organize the words in my head. "What I would say is that—"

Suddenly the doorbell was ringing. The gray-haired man came running down the stairs with a new sense of urgency about him. He asked me to step aside and threw open the front door. Next thing, two EMTs with a gurney entered the townhouse.

"This way, this way, this way," the gray-haired man was shouting.

The EMTs and the gray-haired man went hustling up the stairs to the fifth floor of the townhouse. I stood there, in the foyer, waiting to see who would be coming down on the gurney. They took forever. They should really be working faster to save this person. And was it Miller? But who else could it be? But then it better not be him. The two EMTs were now coming down the stairs with the man on the gurney. They seemed to be using all their strength maneuvering and shifting the gurney from one angle to another, knocking into the banister and the wall, and descending the stairs step by step by step. The man on the gurney was indeed Miller. He was unconscious. The EMTs got him out the door and into an ambulance waiting at the curb. The gray-haired man didn't get into the ambulance with them. He returned inside, fixed the collar of his black suit jacket, took a deep breath, and then turned to me.

"My apologies. *Now*, what was your message for Mr. Miller?"

28

Holding Open a Door

It was the night of Celia's group show at the gallery. After writing down the pros and cons of attending, I concluded that I had to be there. If I didn't go, it could very well be the end of our relationship and one of us might be moving out the next day. I couldn't accept that. I had to show up—for Celia, for Waylon. I was still committed to our relationship and to working through all this hardship and getting to a better place. I had meant it when I told Celia's father, D.W., that I wanted to spend my whole life with her, to be buried next to her—and I still meant it. We would get through this. I would, yes. For Celia, for Waylon, I would get through anything.

Though Celia had never liked me to watch her dress to go out, I did so now from a seat at the end of our bed. I didn't stare, my eye didn't trace her every movement. But I was observing—observing as she slid into her new blue velvet suit, applied her red lipstick, brushed her dark, chin-length hair. She was as beautiful as ever. I could almost imagine she was getting dressed for me, that she still wanted to look good—again—*for me*.

When we pulled up outside the gallery in the taxi, though, it was Dom who opened the door to the car and gave Celia her hand, helping her out onto the street. A white linen suit, white undershirt, white tennis sneakers, her blonde shoulder length hair slicked back. Had she been told *no lips*, not tonight, not in front of me? She didn't kiss Celia on the mouth but awkwardly on the brow. Perhaps she had also been instructed not to make eye contact with me or to say hello. In any event, she did neither, instead heading straight into the gallery with Celia, hand in hand. No doubt Dom had been forced into this, too. *Talked into* it, that is. Therefore, Dom and I were more aligned than Dom would ever like to think, and she shouldn't feel the need to keep her distance. She, too, had been asked to do just this *one more* thing for Celia on this ever-important night, to make one last sacrifice, to accept one more unacceptable situation.

She, too.

She, too.

She, too.

No one had held the door to the gallery open for me. I waited there for a moment on the sidewalk. For what? I didn't know. For strength or a reason to intercede or simply for a friend to walk inside with. On cue, Graham made his way up the block in a tweed suit, a bouquet of flowers in one hand. From a distance he seemed almost like someone arriving at his own big night and that this could have been *his* tremendous break, the one he had been working toward for over ten years. Then the closer he came to me, the more I could tell that he was not doing so well at all. The suit was fine, the flowers attractive, but his eyes were bloodshot and his coloring almost green. He was shaky, sweating, very thin. I had heard something about him having lost his job, too. The flowers had cost him all the money he had left to his name, probably.

"For me?" I said, reaching for the bouquet.

Graham smiled. "Sorry, my good friend. These are for the star of the night."

"Celia will love them."

"I hope so."

We lingered in silence. More taxis pulled up at the curb and people hustled into the gallery: Anne Noel and her husband, Leon, the gallerist, Niles, all dressed up and no doubt ready to jump on Celia's bandwagon.

"Is Nicole coming tonight?" I asked.

Graham lowered his head, gently kicking the toe of his wingtip shoe at the sidewalk. "Afraid to say it, but we're not together anymore, Paul."

"Oh, no. I'm sorry to hear that."

"Me, too. Nicole's a great person. I like her so much. Alas, maybe I let her slip away. I don't know. But tonight we're here to celebrate Celia. Are you ready? I'm going to head in. What do you say?"

"Ah, yes. You first," I told him.

I opened the door for Graham, and he walked in. I was about to follow him, but just before that could happen, a down-and-out man half-dragging his body up the sidewalk appeared. He was shouting at me. With his long wild dark hair and button-down shirt open, chest exposed, the cuffs of his pants shredded, sneakers caked in dirt—he was pointing at me, yes, nodding, seriously, vehemently, saying:

"Shit man, hell, that guy's got a major medical condition. He a friend of yours? Call a physician. He needs a doctor. You get a look at that face? He's in trouble. Big, big trouble, man."

"Who's that?" I said.

"The fella with the flowers. You see that guy? He looked *bad*. Like he was at death's door. Get that man to a hospital."

"What's that?"

"I've seen many go in my day. That guy, that guy, that guy, *wow*. You got a phone. Call 911. He needs fluids. He needs a steak. He needs a hot bath."

"Oh, okay. Thank you," I said. "We'll look after him. It's okay. Thank you."

The man continued mumbling to himself down the block.

The taxi Celia and I had taken here was still parked at the curb. I lunged for the car door and caught it just as it was beginning to pull out. I apologized to the driver. I needed him to turn around and take me right back home.

"I'm sorry," I said. "Is that okay? Can you drive me? I'm so glad I caught you. Oh God, you don't even know. Thank you, thank you."

The Cursed Corners Diary

Curse, did you hear? Celia's show was a great success. The large painting of Dom sold to an important collector for $30,000. The gallery has scheduled her solo show for the fall. There's already a waiting list for new works. Can you imagine that? And can you imagine that Celia is also meeting with a realtor tomorrow to find a new apartment? Did you know about that? You did, didn't you? Because you drew up her exit. You're so predictable. But then, so am I. Today I walk around the city and all I see everywhere I look is cursed corners, cursed corners, cursed corners. More and more cursed corners.

29
Riding Off

I decided to buy Waylon a new bicycle. Probably he had outgrown his last. Bringing him to the bike shop and allowing him to pick out a new bicycle was a mostly constructive way of passing the hours Celia, Graham, and Dom would spend moving Celia's things out of the apartment. Waylon didn't have to witness his mother's life being boxed up and bagged and loaded into the back of a car. He would do much better in a bike shop, selecting a new model.

Right after the blue dirt bike was paid for, we went to the park along the East River in Williamsburg so he could do some riding. He pedaled off the moment we arrived and now I couldn't find him. Was he missing? After just two minutes? Not likely. And yet I regretted having not flagged the last police car. My son could be anywhere. How long before I should call Celia and tell her? But what would I even say? That on the very day she had moved out, I had gone and lost our son? I wouldn't dare. He was exploring. He would turn up.

The park felt impossibly large, expansive beyond reason. I held an image in my mind's eye of Celia and I at the local precinct, seated in wooden chairs at a desk, expressions of loss on our faces. But no, Waylon wasn't gone-gone. And if he were, he wasn't gone forever. There was no chance of that. He would turn up. He was here. He *had* to be. But what if he wasn't? What if he was already in the back of some car—and *no*. He was here. I just had to find him.

"Waylon! Waylon! Hey, Waylon!"

Nothing.

I could feel my phone vibrating. It was Celia. I wouldn't pick up. But then I was supposed to hand Waylon off to her later today and what if I hadn't found him in time? What if he never turned up again? What if the rest of my life were dedicated to searching for my son? Because he had been taken, abducted, stolen from me in a split moment, a moment I could have prevented had I not let him speed away from me on his brand-new bicycle, a bicycle that I had only bought for him to limit his exposure to the awful, traumatic experience of seeing his mother pack up her things from his home—our home—and load them into a car and—

Salvation.

There he was, my son, emerging from a pack of some ten children, sobbing, the strap of his bicycle helmet reining in a quivering chin. "Dad! Dad!" he shouted. The child dropped his new dirt bike and ran straight into my arms. "Oh, Dad!"

"Waylon!"

"Dad!" he said, weeping. "Dad, I was so scared. Where were you?"

"I was looking for you, of course. Where'd you go?"

But it wasn't easy for the child to speak, he was crying so hard.

"We must have just missed each other," I said. Kneeling, I brought my arms around him, kissed his face, the boy's tears wet on my cheek. "Waylon, you can't just go off like that."

"I know. I didn't mean to. I just turned around and you were gone, Dad."

I squeezed the child against my chest again. "It's okay, Waylon. It's my fault. I shouldn't have let you get away. I should have kept up. I'm sorry."

—

I didn't like to read too deeply into incidents like Waylon riding off on his bike and getting himself lost, but I couldn't help myself. Celia and I had spoken to him about his mother moving out as a non-thing. No one cried or screamed or said that life was even being disrupted. But Waylon was a smart child, knew something serious was unfolding around him, and because he had all these feelings that had to come out somewhere, he'd gotten himself lost. No? It seemed plausible.

The night before, Celia and Waylon had slept at her new apartment. In an hour, I was expected over there for breakfast. I would have to see Celia and our son together in an apartment where I did not live, and could there be anything worse?

Celia let me in. Having showered, she was wearing a navy bathrobe that we had shared since before Waylon's birth. The apartment was comfortable, though small, just two rooms: a kitchen and bedroom. The window in the bathroom was cracked and couldn't be locked. Was it safe here? Who was the landlord? Did Celia know anything about him? I had to trust that Waylon and Celia would be all right in *this* apartment? We still didn't know who had written me the threatening letters. Perhaps that person would show up here. The possibility of this haunted me.

Celia was preparing breakfast, chopping apples, ladling yogurt into mismatched bowls. She called to Waylon and said that he should shut the television.

"Did Dom sleep here last night?"

"Sleep in the one bed with me and Waylon? *No.*"

"Will she ever?"

"Not on Waylon's nights."

Waylon's nights? The ease with which she had said it hurt me terribly.

Over breakfast, Celia asked Waylon if there was anything he wanted to talk about. "Anything you're feeling about your mom and dad living in different places that you want to tell us?"

"Anything you're sad about?" I said.

"No," said Waylon. "I love this place. We're right above Angelo's."

Angelo's was his favorite slice in the city. The smell of pizza came up through the floors. I was grateful Waylon could find a positive in this. The child stood now, placed his bowl in the sink, and left the room.

"We're not done talking," his mother told him. "Come back."

Waylon returned at once, his long brown hair in his eyes, and went to sit in his mother's lap.

"We just want to make sure you know that you can tell us anything," said Celia.

"I know."

"We love you so much," she said.

"I know you do."

"There's nothing you can't tell us or that will ever make us love you less," Celia said.

"I know, Mom." At the next moment, though, Waylon popped out of his mother's arms and disappeared into the bedroom.

I didn't stay much longer, only a few minutes. I couldn't bear being here. When it was time for me to leave, Celia called out to Waylon to say goodbye to his dad. The child came running from the bedroom, brown eyes gleaming. In the doorway, Waylon brought his arms around my waist.

"Goodbye, Dad."

"Bye, Waylon. I love you."

"I love you."

Celia watched us from a few feet away. Was she waiting for the child to let go of me? I wasn't sure he would. But then I squatted to match his height, put my hands to his cheeks. At once I noted something in Waylon's expression that was trying to encourage me, a quality behind his eyes that said it was okay. I had never seen this look from my son before.

"You have a good day with your mom," I said.

"Thanks, Dad. Bye-bye." But Waylon didn't move. "I love you," he said.

"I love you, too. I'll see you the day after tomorrow."

"Okay," said Waylon. His arms tightened around me. "I love you, Dad."

My child was going to make me cry. "Go have a very good day with your mother. I love you, too. I'll see you in two days."

Waylon and I let go of one another and with a brief wave to his mother, our expressions flattened by the impossibility of the situation, I hurried down the stairwell and across the street. I waited until I was part-way up the block, brought my face inside my coat, and wept.

30
A Mother's Goodbye

"...Men vigorously pursued my mother. She was attractive, successful, and only in her mid-thirties when she and my father split. But she didn't want these men around. She was not, as some might say, emotionally available. She couldn't bring herself to have feelings for them. And, unsurprisingly, this drove many of them to want her that much more and to come after her with all the more energy. How many afternoons did I arrive home from school to be presented by the doorman with another bouquet of flowers or box of chocolates for my mother? Who could even count. Packages of all kinds were always showing up at the door—televisions and kitchen appliances and antique furniture, jewels, trips, mink coats—it didn't stop. Nothing was ever sent back. And yet my mother could get very upset at the arrival of another gift from such and such person. I might knock on her bedroom door and tell her that Joel or Phil or Kevin or Steve had sent her more flowers, and she would become irate. She had told him to leave her alone. She would call that one a pest. She had practically begged this one to lose her number. What was wrong with these men? Couldn't they get it through their heads that she wasn't interested? I had to talk to many of them on the phone. It would not be fair to my mother to say that I would have to break up with them for her. She would have already done this, often more than once. But I would have to bring the message home—reiterate— that she had no interest in another date and that more and more gifts were not helping their cause. It wasn't difficult for me as much as it was embarrassing, painfully so. I felt for these men. I could hear how deeply they wanted to see my mother again, to have another chance. But my mother would be waving two hands before her face, insisting that I please handle the call because this one on the line induced nausea in her. I would have to let them down easily. Or, I wouldn't have to, but if it seemed appropriate, necessary, as if the man deserved some kindness. I would choose my words carefully. I would tell them she had been so busy at work or that she was not socializing much of late, anything to ease the impact of her rejection…"

I was at the Carlyle Hotel, standing at my mother's table, waiting for this Jacob, the new waiter, to take a goddamn breath and get up from my seat and give me my mother. My mother was telling him to go on, to tell her *everything*. She hadn't said anything to Jacob about the fact that I was here to see her, that I was her son, that he was in my seat. Instead, in her gold sparking day dress, her blonde hair blown out, voluminous, she was saying:

"That must have been so hard, Jacob."

"It was, it was so *so* hard," said Jacob, seeming to hold back tears.

"Mom, do you think you two could wrap this up?"

"Where do you have to be?" said my mother.

She was right. I had no appointments.

Mercifully, Jacob's boss came to my aid and encouraged him to return to work. Of course, everyone would like to sit with my mother and talk to her all day, his boss acknowledged, but there was a job to be done. Jacob apologized to my mother and walked off. I sat down across from her.

"Fred, can I have some more lemon, please?"

"Why yes, my dear," said Fred, with a smile and a nod.

"I've never seen a guy so happy to get a person lemon, Mom. How do you do it?"

"I *listen* to them, Paul. That's how. I listen and I listen, and I do not judge."

"That must be nice," I said, opening a menu.

My mother's plate of lemon wedges appeared. She squeezed them one by one into a cup of tea, her light eyes narrowing with the effort of her long fingers. "This is the worst of it, honey. You'll feel better soon."

"I don't know."

"*I know*. I've been there before. How's Waylon? Okay? That boy looks like her, yes, but he has *your* heart. How do I know? Because she doesn't have one, does she?"

"Well—"

"Listen, find yourself a good hotel, move right in. That's what I recommend."

"Mom, I don't even have a job right now. I have to find a new one."

"So I hear. I hope you're happy to be moving on from your newsletter."

"No. It was the greatest job in the world."

"The greatest job? Paul, no. Get a grip, please. Anyway, there's something I need to tell you and the fact is, what I'm going to say will not make you very happy. But what I did was necessary. Yes, it was good for you. It was something you needed in a very bad way."

"What are you talking about, Mom?"

My mother sat up even taller in her chair. "Those letters, the ones that...you know...the, the, the...what do you want to call them...the death threats...that was me. I wrote them. You're welcome. It was the least I could do for you. Oh, come on, don't cry. Keep it together. It was no big deal. Jacob, water, please. This man needs water!"

Jacob placed a full glass of water in front of me. I couldn't take the glass in my hand. I couldn't even breathe. "Did you just say you wrote those letters, Mom? What the hell do you mean!"

"Hey, hey, don't raise your voice at me. I carried you, I birthed you, I raised you."

"Mom, what are you saying you've done? Did you really do it? Did you really write those letters?"

"You have to get a *real* job, Paul, a better job. That newsletter—it was some kind of fantasy you were living."

"And what do you call all this!" I said, pointing in every which direction.

"*This* is a life. You can't be a newsletter writer forever. You have a child to support. You need to do something more substantial, better paying."

"Mom, that newsletter was not *just* a newsletter. I was making change."

"No, baby. No, you weren't. Honestly, I couldn't even understand what any of it was about."

"Cursed corners, Mom. It was about cursed—"

My mother held up a hand. She seemed as if she were about to tell me something important, maybe personal to her own life. It turned out that Fred was sliding in and around the table behind me and my mother needed more lemon.

"Thank you, Fred. Just a few more wedges would be great. Maybe more than a few. Oh, just give me the whole lemon."

The Cursed Corners Diary, a Final Note

Dear Curse,

The fact is, I can't stop thinking and talking about you. And then I have this awful need to write about you, too. Are you okay with that? Are you sure? Would you like me to pick another phenomenon? My mother says I must. But you have to be recognized, wouldn't you agree? Without doing so—without speaking up about you—we might just let all of New York City become...well...cursed.

But Curse, let me ask you:

If there's no such thing as permanence, does that mean we shouldn't still dream of making things that last? The identity of our city requires a certain amount of belief in forever, does it not? But then nothing is forever. So, how do you reconcile this? By leaving things empty, yes. Well, we all see your empty corners—see and feel them.

But maybe now that I've proven my devotion to you, you'll tell me how to break the curse? Say a word or two about it? Or how about I stop putting you on the spot for the moment. But tell me, where else are you holding pain? We should at least talk about it. 54th Street and Seventh Avenue? Lafayette and Bleecker? Park Avenue and 25th Street? You can tell me about each and every ache. I want to know. I, myself, will never stop taking note. But did you hear? I'm writing a book about your corners far and wide, from those here in New York, throughout the country and across the world. London, Tokyo, Berlin, Paris—I hope to set out next month. Sometimes I'm kept up at night by a concern for those corners that I'll miss and sometimes I dream about those corners I'll come upon in the most unusual of places. Curse, I'll see you out there. Yes, yes, yes. If there's one thing I know, it's that you'll be waiting for me, hiding in plain sight.

Acknowledgments

Thank you...

Tyson Cornell, my constant supporter, Guy Intoci, my brilliant editor, Hailie Johnson, and everyone at Rare Bird.

W.M. Akers—always, always, my friend.

To my early readers Tyler Wetherall, Alex Gilvarry, Paula Bomber, Matthew Binder, Michelle Savitt (my mom), and Robert Tepper (my dad)—thank you for your invaluable notes and encouragement.

To those who published *Cooler Heads* in early form, in chronological order: Taylor Plimpton (*Manhattan Magazine*), Will Chancellor (*The Brooklyn Rail*), and Anika Jade Levy and Madeline Cash (*Forever Magazine*). Writing and publishing a novel takes so much time and effort. To be able to share excerpts with the reading public along the way was a great salve.

Thank you to my brothers and friends—you know who you are—and again to my parents, who carried me through a deep and hellish valley, and without whom I likely would not have made it. I love you.

And finally, thank you to my wife, Paige, and my sons, Silas and Augie, my *raison d'etre*.

About the Author

Julian Tepper is the author of the novels *Balls, Ark, Between the Records,* and *Cooler Heads*. His work has appeared in *The Paris Review, Playboy Magazine, Tablet Magazine, The Daily Beast, The Brooklyn Rail, Zyzzyva, Mr. Beller's Neighborhood,* and elsewhere. He co-founded the Oracle Club, a literary salon in New York City that operated from 2011–2017. He was born on April 1, 1979, and raised on the Upper East Side of Manhattan.

Printed in the USA
CPSIA information can be obtained
at www.ICGtesting.com
JSHW031509301223
53928JS00001B/1/J